# Saddle a Dream

ALSO BY BRENDA SINCLAIR

Carsen Family Trilogy
Tangled Heartstrings, Tangled Memories, Tangled Intentions

The Spirit Creek Series
Historical Western Romance
No More, No Time, No Chance, No Ties,
No Peace (Novella), No Way, No Hope

Escape to Alaska Trilogy
Not What It Seems, Almost Doesn't Count, Never A Bride

A Bandit Creek Miracle
When Dreams Collide (Sequel to A Bandit Creek Miracle)

Part of the Thurston Hotel Series
A Thurston Promise, A Thurston Christmas

Love to the Rescue
50% of the author's royalties donated to
Humane Society shelters

Stampede Sizzlers
Cooking For Cowboy, Secrets For Cowboy

# Saddle a Dream

## A WOMEN OF STAMPEDE NOVEL

WℓS

## BRENDA SINCLAIR

*Dream Big!*

*BSinclair*

Published June 2018 by Brenda Sinclair
ISBN 978-1-926474-17-5 (Print edition)

Design and cover art by Su Kopil, Earthly Charms
Copyediting by Ted Williams

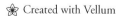 Created with Vellum

# DEDICATION

*To my fellow Women of Stampede authors.*
*You've made this project so much fun.*

# ACKNOWLEDGMENTS

Firstly, a special thank you to Shelley Kassian and Katie O'Connor for inviting me to join this fabulous group of authors who created the Women of Stampede Series. It has been a pleasure working with every one of you. And thank you to Vicki, Katie and Shelley for beta reading my initial drafts. Thank you Jan for your assistance and beta reading the medical scenes. Thank you also to Su Kopil from www.earthlycharms.com for this wonderful cover. And thank you to Ted Williams for line editing.

A special thank you to the people who helped with my research. Thank you to Michelle Jacobs from the Tsuut'ina Nation for providing invaluable insight into the life of a Tsuut'ina woman and information on volunteering at the Indian Village during Stampede. I enjoyed the conversation and the laughter shared with you. And thank you to Hal Eagletail, a Culture Advisor for the Tsuut'ina Nation, for sharing your knowledge of the Tsuut'ina history, and answering my many questions. I greatly appreciate your assistance with my research.

A special thank you to Executive Sous Chef Will Kwong from Stampede Catering for the tour of banquet halls, staff room and kitchens, and for answering dozens of questions about the duties and responsibilities of the chefs and other staff. I could not have written this book without your help! Stampede Catering is a wonderful organization that generously provides student chefs, including my granddaughter, with invaluable hands-on experience and on-the-job training as they pursue their chosen careers. Thank you, Cassidy Sinclair, for your help during the writing of this book by answering endless questions. Lastly but of equal importance, thank you to Marilyn Ross for sharing her experiences as a Stampede volunteer. It's folks like you, Marilyn, who help make Stampede the success it continues to be!

Of course, any errors within this book are mine alone.

# CHAPTER 1

Calgary, Canada
Third Tuesday in June

*L*ydia Simpson-Crowchild entered the two connecting halls in the BMO Centre on the Stampede grounds, where a buzz of conversation peppered with frequent bouts of laughter greeted her.

With several thousand people in attendance, the room was bursting at the seams with volunteers, their guests and exhibition staff seated at tables for the annual Saddle Up dinner. As an experienced part-time server with Stampede Catering, Lydia loved working all events, especially this get-together in preparation for the start of the Calgary Stampede. Clasping a round, rubber-lined tray in her hands, she maneuvered around people making their way to their tables, dinner plates heaped with the delectable culinary masterpieces served at the various buffet stations along the far wall.

Out of the corner of her eye, she noticed the handsome sous chef she'd been dying to meet working at one of the entree stations, carving a serving of top round beef for a volunteer. Warren Chamberland smiled broadly, interacting with the guests he served and with his co-worker and fellow sous chef, Nick.

Lydia cleared away dirty dishes from a table, but soon caught herself glancing at Warren again. She'd forfeit a week's wages for the opportunity to run her fingers through his short, wavy brown hair. To touch his neatly trimmed beard and tidy moustache, two of his best features. But those eyes! She'd caught him watching her. Deliberately. Intensely. Shamelessly. And he'd smile at her before returning to his work. When he looked at her like that, her heart beat faster and his chocolate brown eyes seemed to peer right into her soul. He looked so sexy, especially in that white chef's coat! Warren exited the room, probably heading to the kitchen.

She sighed and resumed her duties. She enjoyed interacting with co-workers and meeting interesting people, whether serving at a high school graduation, an elegant wedding at the Lazy S or the Palomino Ballroom, or tonight's volunteer appreciation dinner. And she'd worked with the handsome chef at a few previous events. Would she ever muster up the courage to introduce herself? How would Warren feel about a First Nations girl? Would he like her? Maybe ask her out on a date?

"Sorry, miss." An older gentleman apologized for bumping into her.

Lydia smiled at him. "That's okay. It gets a bit crowded in here at times." According to information she'd read on the Calgary Stampede website, over 2,300 volunteers helped with the many facets of the Exhibition organization. And every one of those volunteers could bring a guest to tonight's appreciation dinner. Even her mother and aunt were seated somewhere. And including the staff, Lydia estimated there could be five thousand people here tonight!

"Thank goodness, I'm not cooking for all of them," she muttered, clearing dirty dishes and glasses from a table where people had vacated their chairs to visit a dessert station.

"These servers are certainly quick to clear the dishes, aren't they?"

"Very efficient," another woman concurred.

Lydia smiled, delighted that the wait staff's efforts were appreciated.

"Dessert to complete and we're finished."

Lydia nodded to the male server working at her side, preoccupied with dozens of thoughts swimming in her head. She could barely wrap her mind around everything on her agenda once the Stampede began.

Head down and distracted, she carried the fully loaded tray to the curtained-off area for cleaning and stacking dirty dishes before transport down the hallway to the dishwashers. Stepping inside, Lydia slammed into a solid wall of tall, handsome man. She quickly executed an epic move—half juggling act and half pirouette—to prevent the tray of dishes from crashing to the floor. A stack of glasses wobbled and then settled back on the tray.

"What the hell?" the man exclaimed. "Pay attention to where you're walking."

Despite having the breath nearly knocked out of her, she realized she'd collided with the handsome sous chef she'd been admiring—all right, ogling—a few minutes ago. Thankfully, Warren hadn't fallen and she hoped he hadn't been hurt by their collision.

"Oh, my goodness. Are you okay? What was I thinking?" she stammered. What the heck was Warren doing here anyway? Hadn't he returned to the kitchen?

She felt her face pale. She didn't know what to do!

"What if I'd been carrying a large pot of steaming hot soup?" Warren grimaced. "Or a 100-cup coffee urn? We'd both have third degree burns!"

Lydia had never seen him annoyed, always the gregarious one in the kitchen. Well, she'd managed to incite his displeasure.

"I was distracted and I'm sorry. It won't happen again." Now she'd done it! She'd been hoping to meet the handsome chef, but certainly not this way. He stared at her. She couldn't imagine what he was thinking. She straightened her shoulders and met his eyes. "What I did was wrong, but no one was hurt. Maybe you're over-reacting."

He hurried out through the curtained doorway, calling over his shoulder, "Saving the dishes… that was an impressive maneuver. But be more careful or you could find yourself out of a job."

Lydia emptied her tray of dishes, scraping the plates and stacking them in one of the wheeled dish caddies. She should have been paying attention. But, oh my god! Warren Chamberland had actually talked to her! And it never would have happened without that chance incident.

"What happened?" Another female server had followed her into the curtained area.

Lydia shook her head. "An unfortunate accident, Barb."

"What accident? Are you hurt?" The forty-something woman resembled a concerned mother as she examined Lydia's hands and face.

"I collided with Warren. When I entered the curtained area, I didn't notice he was exiting."

"Oh, no. Are you okay?"

Lydia nodded.

"Was he hurt?"

"I don't think so. But he was ticked off. I hope I still have a job."

"Did Warren threaten to fire you?"

"No, and I don't think he can fire me. Only the catering supervisor can. Or the person who hired me, or… I don't know." Lydia's shoulders slumped as she finished clearing her tray. "I hope it doesn't happen."

Barb met her eyes. "Why did you collide with Warren?"

"I was completely distracted by my thoughts."

"Trouble at home?" Barb speculated as her face paled. "Oh, no. Is someone ill? Are you?"

Lydia shook her head. "No! Nothing like that. I was worried about the upcoming days."

"Stampede is always a crazy time." Barb stacked the plates from her tray onto a dish caddy.

"I'm hoping I don't have a double-booking," Lydia confessed.

"They wouldn't double-book you to serve."

"Oh, Barb, I'm not worried about that. Stampede Catering is excellent at scheduling." Lydia shifted her weight onto her other foot. "It's my mother's doing. She volunteered me for a dozen things and told me about them after the fact. And besides my shifts here, I'll be participating in the Stampede Parade, representing the Tsuut'ina nation."

"Really?"

"My mother is a Tsuut'ina member. I compete at powwows, and I'll be performing in the parade." Lydia also looked forward to the upcoming First Nations competitions with anticipation. Teepee raising and powwow dancing, the latter of which she'd competed in since age ten. "I'll be assisting with my nations' open teepee presentation in the Indian Village, helping to set up the display of hides, beadwork and crafts, travois, headdresses, tools, weaponry and other items. All of which will be judged in the General Inspection by the Stampede Board."

"That sounds wonderful." Barb appeared truly interested.

Lydia met her co-worker's eyes. "You should cross the bridge to the entrance to the Indian Village and wander around."

"I'll do that." Barb smiled.

"Mom signed me up to help the elders, including my grandfather, with storytelling. And to volunteer for several shifts at the Bannock Booth. And to aid any of the First Nations vendors who might need assistance. Lord knows what else. My University of Calgary roommate wants me to accompany her to the midway a few nights. We have tickets for one day's rodeo and the chuckwagon races on Wednesday. And we have Luke Bryan concert tickets for Saturday night." Lydia sighed loudly. "Honestly, I have no idea how I'll fit it all in."

"One thing at a time," Barb reasoned, patting her arm.

"I guess so. Come on. We'll both be fired if we don't get back to work." Empty trays in their hands, Lydia followed Barb into the event room.

Lydia continued clearing tables and assisting guests who required directions to the nearest washrooms, despite the clear signage throughout the room. Troubling thoughts crept into her mind. Silently fuming over all the commitments her mother had initiated on her behalf, she caught herself being unduly rough with the dishware. She inhaled deeply and took greater care with the dishes.

Her grandfather had attempted to discuss the matter with her mother, suggesting Lydia be allowed to do her own thing and to enjoy Stampede with her friends. Grandfather might as well have saved his breath for all the good it had done. Her mother had volunteered at Stampede and worked at the Indian Village for years, and she'd set her mind on Lydia following in her footsteps.

Lydia returned to the curtained-off area once again, head up and paying attention, nonetheless still feeling completely overwhelmed. Thankfully, she'd recorded everything on her schedule in her cell phone, praying she wouldn't discover a duplication or forget something. Worst of all, she hadn't begun to consider whether or not she should bother returning to the U of C next fall for the final year of her degree. Considering the challenging third year of nurse's training she'd completed, especially the practical work with actual patients, she'd questioned whether a career as a registered nurse was right for her.

She hoped she didn't encounter Warren again tonight.

One scolding was plenty.

~

WARREN CHAMBERLAND EXITED the curtained area where he'd been looking for the catering supervisor with a message that one of his servers had gone home ill. Before colliding with Lydia, he'd intended to check how tonight's attendees were enjoying their desserts.

He took a deep breath and wandered across the room to stand near where guests were passing through the dessert stations. One of the student pastry chefs had utilized red fruit gel to create the Stampede logo as an additional element to the plating. The young woman's initiative impressed him, and he was curious about the guests' reactions. Several diners offered favorable comments on the lovely presentation to the chefs standing nearby. The young chef responsible for the creative addition blushed at so many guests' exuberant praise. Warren smiled; they hadn't tasted the chocolate delicacy yet, won over by presentation alone. Another successful Saddle Up dinner neared completion.

His back ached and his feet hurt; he hadn't felt this tired in days. Thank goodness, they'd finalized all of the high school graduations for the year. Recently having catered three in one day had been a bit much, but the staff had survived the hectic graduation season. After tonight's dinner, the next major event would be the wedding reception in the Palomino Ballroom this coming Saturday. Some government fellow's daughter was marrying a doctor's son. Big news, apparently. Warren only cared about the menu which would be legendary if they pulled it off. And they would. They always did.

One advantage to working for Stampede Catering, he'd been learning from some of the best chefs in the field. He'd aced the Red Seal exam just prior to being hired here as sous chef. With each shift under these gentlemen's tutelage, Warren moved closer to his dream job: landing the position of executive chef at the Fairmont Palliser in downtown Calgary. Or somewhere similar. But he'd be keeping that goal to himself. His best friend and fellow sous chef, Nick Jackson, would enjoy razzing him about it. Nick planned to travel the world and work on cruise ships. And he'd hoped Warren would accompany him on his adventures. Not happening.

Just thinking about all the events and guests they'd be cooking for during Stampede made his heartbeat race. Between the upscale venues like The Lazy S and ranahans and places like the Clubhouse, the Rangeland Tent, the Wine Garden and Rotary House and several others, the entire staff would be run off their feet. He couldn't wait! He loved nothing better than a challenge!

Warren's thoughts wandered to what had occurred a few minutes ago, despite attempting to relegate the incident to the farthest recesses of his mind. But how could he forget? Especially the other person involved. He'd noticed the Indigenous server, had caught her staring at him a few times. *Lydia*. Pretty name for a gorgeous woman who looked a bit younger than him. Constantly smiling, she goofed around a lot when preparing for a shift. He'd learned that she'd been employed with Stampede Catering every summer for several years now, and Lydia was an excellent server, despite her carefree ways.

What had caused her inattentive behavior tonight?

Would her supervisor fire her?

And why did she have to look so damn cute?

Big brown eyes sparkling with mischief and dark chestnut hair which hung down her back, secured by some kind of jewel-encrusted clip and covered by a hairnet. His gaze had roamed her slim body, pausing at her full breasts and moving downward past her hips. She looked good dressed in those black pants and black collared shirt, with the mandatory Stampede apron tied around her slim waist, accentuating her curves. While he'd chastised her with his face inches from hers, the enticing scent that enveloped her sexy body had sent his olfactory senses into overdrive.

He imagined how sexy she'd look in a little black dress and heels, each step she took toward him causing those long strands of silky hair to bounce about her shoulders. Reluctantly, he shook that image from his mind and forced his thoughts back on track.

The young woman he'd reprimanded had appeared remorseful. He'd only been doing his job. He'd considered her one of their best servers. Had he been wrong? And he'd heard she was training as a nurse. Was she cut out for a life-or-death career like nursing?

But why did he care?

Getting involved with a woman was the last thing he needed with his life's goal this close in sight. If he could only keep those beautiful eyes off his mind.

# CHAPTER 2

*H*ours later, Lydia stepped outside and inhaled the warm night air, intent on walking to her vehicle and driving home. She'd shed the black pants and shirt in favor of dark skinny-jeans and a lacy white sweater.

She wanted to forget this night had ever happened! This evening's shift had seemed never-ending, especially after her encounter with Warren. Although stunned by her carelessness, she shouldn't have accused him of overreacting; he'd been right to chastise her. Word of what had happened would travel to the catering supervisor, if he hadn't heard already, perhaps numbering her days as a server. She shouldn't have allowed her worries to interfere with her work.

She removed the clip from the back of her head and stuffed it into an outside pocket of her purse. A breeze ruffled the long strands of her hair as she shook them loose.

"Hey!" Warren called, stepping out of the building. The door closed behind him.

Hearing his footsteps moving closer, Lydia turned around and faced him. Why must he look so handsome? Six feet tall, slim and fit. She'd love to feel his trimmed beard pressed against her cheek. If he kissed her would his moustache tickle? She'd felt an immediate attraction to the chef the first time she'd spotted him at an event and she'd wanted to meet him for a while now.

Well, she'd certainly met him!

"We've never actually been introduced. I'm Warren Chamberland." He zipped up his light summer jacket.

She forced a smile. "Hi. Lydia Simpson-Crowchild."

They shook hands.

"Lydia… I need to apologize."

"No apology necessary. I was totally in the wrong and I know better. As I said, it will *never* happen again." Her fingers tingled from contact with his warm hand.

"Regardless, I didn't act professionally and I'm sorry." He hooked each thumb through a belt loop on his jeans.

"You had every right to call me out for my carelessness," Lydia insisted.

"You mentioned you were distracted." He shook his head. "Must have been some distraction."

"Thinking about things instead of doing the job I was paid to do." Lydia grimaced. "I've learned my lesson the hard way, letting my problems cloud my concentration."

"Big problems?" One eyebrow rose.

Lydia laughed. "Not really. I wasn't planning strategies for world peace. Just personal stuff."

Warren chuckled and met her eyes. "Would you like to go for coffee somewhere before heading home? Maybe we could solve some of these problems, if you care to share."

Lydia shook her head. "It's pretty late, but thank you for the invitation. No serious problems. I'm a little overwhelmed with my busy schedule."

Warren unhooked his thumbs from the belt loops and stared at her for a few moments. "Maybe another time then."

Lydia dug her keys out of her purse. He sounded disappointed. Should she have turned him down? Would he ask her out again another night? To coffee? To dinner? He'd graciously accepted that she'd declined his invitation. Most guys she encountered would try every trick in their repertoire to talk her into a date. Perhaps Warren's invitation was a matter of him being polite.

"Let me walk you to your car," he offered, taking a step closer. "I'm parked in the lot a couple blocks over."

Lydia smiled. "I'm parked there, too. Thank you for offering. It's perfectly safe, but I'd enjoy the company." She gazed into his eyes, realizing how close to her he stood. His expression revealed conflicting emotions, none of which she could put a name to. She swallowed, her mouth dry. If she leaned a little closer, would he kiss her? She couldn't move a muscle.

"Okay." He returned her smile and took a step back.

Together, they walked toward their vehicles. After a few steps, Warren placed his hand at her back, silently guiding her in the dim illumination from the light standards, ensuring her safety should she stumble. His warm touch burned her skin through her lacy sweater. For a moment, she considered tripping on purpose, hoping he'd wrap his arms around her.

Tomorrow, Lydia could find herself fired from her favorite part-time job. Of course, she'd have no one to blame but herself. If that happened, she might never see Warren again.

Darn it. She should have accepted his invitation to coffee!

ON HIS WAY to the parking lot, walking alongside Lydia, Warren wished he hadn't been so quick to chastise her earlier. No harm had come to either of them. Heck, she hadn't even dropped one dish. How she'd managed that maneuver remained a mystery; he could never match the talent with a tray that the servers displayed. Had he overreacted?

No, he'd only been doing his job. Was she annoyed with him? Was that why she hadn't accepted his invitation to coffee? Without thinking, he placed his hand at her back. Heat raced up his arm the moment he touched her; he'd swear he could feel her skin through the lacy top she wore. The sidewalk wasn't well-lit and he didn't want her to fall. He caught himself smiling. That was his story, and he was sticking to it.

His eyes strained in the darkness, as he tried to read her expression. Was she smiling? Had she forgiven him for that remark about losing her job? Why couldn't his muddled brain think of anything for him to say?

Lydia led him to a dark gray SUV which appeared no more than a year or two old. Part-time servers made minimum wage. And being a university student, how could Lydia afford that ride? Unless she'd won a lottery or signed up for seven years of debt. Being a student, she probably wouldn't qualify for the latter.

Had someone loaned it to her? Maybe a parent paid for it? Or a husband? For some reason, *that* possibility didn't sit well with him. Lydia wasn't wearing a diamond or a wedding ring, but some servers didn't wear their best jewelry at work. And with her hyphenated surname… Lets face it, this was none of his damn business.

When Lydia turned and faced him, his hand lost contact with her back and dropped to his side.

"Thank you for seeing me safely to my vehicle," she offered, smiling.

"You're welcome," he croaked; his throat tightened and he realized he'd unknowingly taken a step closer. And then of its own volition, his hand reached out and touched her cheek. So warm. So soft. Lydia inhaled sharply. His hand stilled. "You're so beautiful." He wanted to kiss her so badly.

"This is not a good idea," she whispered, as if reading his mind, but she leaned closer to him.

"Probably not."

She closed her eyes and a second later, he tentatively brushed her lips with his.

A sigh escaped her.

He deepened the kiss, wrapped his arms around her, and gently eased her against him. His heart nearly stopped, sensations from their kiss rampaging through every nerve in his body. Was she experiencing something similar? And, oh my, could Lydia kiss! He certainly didn't regret initiating the idea. All too soon, she ended the kiss, leaning back and staring into his eyes.

Warren dragged one hand through his hair. "*Not a good idea,* you said. God help me, woman, if you ever kiss me when you do consider it a good idea. My heart may not survive."

She laughed. "We could do it again. If you're willing to risk it."

"Hell, yeah." A fire ignited as Warren repeated the kiss. Lydia matched his ardor and pressed her body against his, wrapping her arms around his neck. She tasted of chocolate and mint; she'd sampled tonight's dessert. All too soon, she ended the kiss, gazing into his eyes. What was she thinking? Had he overstepped boundaries?

"I… I…" he stammered. Her kiss had knocked him senseless.

"Yeah," she replied, appearing equally shocked. "Um… goodnight."

"Goodnight." He took a step back before he tossed reason aside and kissed her yet again.

Lydia touched his arm and then climbed into her vehicle. "I hope I'll see you at another event." She closed the door before his brain slipped into gear.

"Count on it," he called, hoping she'd hear through her closed window.

She nodded, started the SUV, and drove away.

Walking to his pickup parked one row over, he mentally kicked himself for allowing Lydia to distract him, recalling his vow to never become side-tracked from his ultimate goal by a woman. No matter how tempted when staring into those gorgeous brown eyes, he needed to keep his sights set on becoming an executive chef. Period.

But tonight, those eyes had been his undoing. They'd been the reason he'd kissed her. He hadn't one regret. But what the hell had he been thinking? What idiot chewed someone out for a careless mistake, and then sealed it with a kiss?

His thoughts returned to his future as he climbed inside and fastened his seatbelt. There'd be plenty of time to find the perfect wife, and purchase the perfect house in the perfect neighborhood, and have perfect children. Well, maybe not the latter, if his kids proved anything like he and his brother had been while growing up. He smiled at the memories that popped into his head. Two trouble-making hellions for whom his father constantly invented chores as punishment for their antics, and his mother fervently claimed would be the death of her.

Warren hadn't seen his parents, or his brother and his family, for ages. All of them, including his two precocious nephews, would come to the Stampede for at least one day. The falling out with his father was years ago, and Warren looked forward to seeing everyone.

Warren steered his truck toward home. Every bone in his body ached from the long day he'd put in. He thought about the cold beer in the fridge and the comfortable bed waiting for him in his one-bedroom apartment. And the image of Lydia's beautiful smile and those kind, brown eyes looking up at him before he kissed her popped into his mind. He wanted to see her again and soon. Not a good idea for a guy dedicated to becoming an executive chef.

Dammit, ignoring his attraction to Lydia might be harder than he'd imagined. If he kissed her again, he and his plans for the future might be doomed.

# CHAPTER 3

Second last Saturday in June

*L*ydia never turned down the opportunity to serve at a wedding reception hosted by Stampede Catering, especially this one. The whole city and the local media had been buzzing with anticipation for months now.

She didn't know the groom, the son of one of Calgary's leading cardiac specialists. But the talented doctor had saved the life of two of her relatives who'd suffered from serious heart issues. Photos of his son's fiancée had been plastered all over the local media, and she had to agree that the exotic Asian beauty, the adopted daughter of a local MLA, would make a stunning bride.

No costs had been spared in planning the reception.

The white and gold themed décor throughout the Palomino Ballroom in the BMO Centre would impress royalty. Flower arrangements were situated everywhere she looked, many of them featuring several varieties of orchids. Lydia's favorite. And the pricey menu had surprised her, no doubt costing the bride's father a small fortune to accommodate the eight hundred guests. But she'd bet

Warren and the other chefs were in their element, preparing such a sumptuous meal.

She hadn't spotted Warren yet. He'd probably be surprised to see her here. She could hardly believe it herself. She hadn't been fired after the unfortunate collision with him several days ago. At least, no one had phoned or texted her about it, so Lydia showed up for work as scheduled. When she exited the staff room earlier, the catering supervisor had casually inquired if she felt at her best today. She'd assured him she did. He'd left his comments at that and walked away. For a moment, she'd felt light-headed with relief, and then gotten down to business with her duties.

Excited conversation spilled into the room, heralding the arrival of the bridal party. Guests milled about in groups, eagerly waiting to extend their congratulations and best wishes to the happy couple.

"Ladies and gentlemen… may I present to you, Mr. and Mrs. Daniel Monroe…"

Lydia took the arrival of the guests of honor as her cue to prepare for serving the first of many courses when everyone would be seated. She turned around in time to catch a glimpse of Warren standing in the ballroom's doorway. He hadn't spotted her yet, deep in conversation with the executive sous chef, their heads bent together over paperwork. She considered turning her back to avoid his gaze, but decided the best course of action was to face him, having to sooner or later. When the executive sous chef ended the conversation and moved away from Warren, she crossed the floor and approached him, heartbeat racing and hands sweating.

"Hi." She wiped her hands on her Stampede apron.

Warren's head whipped up. He fumbled the sheets of paper in his hand, making a quick recovery before they could flutter to the floor. "You're working here tonight?"

She considered teasing him. *No, I've been stalking you. Haven't you noticed?* But then she thought better of it. She nodded her head. A few seconds later, she added, "Yeah, I am. Should be quite the event."

"That it should. I've got to tend to a few things." Warren smiled briefly and then turned into the hallway.

She stared at his retreating back. That was it?

Soon, Lydia found herself too busy to spare Warren a moment's thought. The reception proved busier than she'd expected, but from the one-bite Asian cuisine appetizers to the choice of either the spicy Tandoori salmon or the shrimp and filet entrées to the variety of decadent desserts, every guest had gushed about the wonderful wedding meal. She couldn't be more proud of everyone who'd contributed to its success.

Lydia and the other servers cleared tables while the bride and groom cut their elegant six-tier cake decorated in edible multi-colored, exotic flowers. And then wandered throughout the room talking to their guests.

When Lydia heard someone giving a speech through a micro-phone, she turned her attention toward the stage. The speaker introduced himself as the brother of the groom and soon had the guests in stitches of laughter while he gave the best man's speech. Members of the band stood off to the side, waiting for their cue. Lydia's gaze fell on the First Nations fellow standing in back of the other four men. He looked familiar. He turned and their eyes met. He smiled and strode across the room.

"Lydia, is that you?"

"Malcolm?" she whispered the name of the boy she'd dated all through high school. She almost didn't recognize him. He'd gained at least thirty pounds, mostly muscle, and he'd grown a foot taller. She used to love his neatly braided hair hanging to his waist, but now his straight, short locks reached just above his shirt collar.

"Yeah, it's me." He smiled at her and hugged her tightly. "Man, I can't believe it. Running into you like this. Weird, huh?"

Lydia laughed. "Yeah, a little weird. What have you been up to?"

He pointed to the stage. "I moved to B.C. and worked various jobs. A couple years ago, I hooked up with this band, *Eagle Feathers*. We're all First Nations except the guy on bass guitar and the lead singer. Waiting for our big break."

"You're in a band?" She gaped. They had sung together in church choirs and high school productions, but she never would have imagined this.

"Drummer. Everyone calls me Sticks." He laughed, the sound bringing back many happy memories of their days together as teens. No one had teased her more, nor sent her heartbeat racing as often either. She recalled their memorable first kiss. She'd secretly loved him with all her heart, a lifetime ago. Until he left the reserve without saying goodbye.

The emcee announced the bride and groom would be sharing their first dance shortly.

"Gotta go. We'll talk later, okay?" he called over his shoulder, heading for the stage.

She nodded and waved before returning to her duties.

A few minutes later, she crossed the ballroom floor with a tray filled with dirty dishes.

"Who was the guy you were talking to?"

Lydia startled, the voice coming from behind her.

She turned and met eyes with Warren. "Oh, hi! He's an old boyfriend from high school. Haven't seen him in years."

"Oh," muttered Warren. "I thought maybe he was bothering you."

"No. Just saying hello," Lydia replied, smiling. "We're you concerned that some guy might be verbally accosting me?" The idea warmed her from head to toe.

"I thought he looked a little sketchy."

Lydia stared at Warren. "I've known him since I was a kid. His name is Malcolm Jack, but apparently everyone calls him Sticks now. He's the band's drummer."

Hearing the band starting to play while the lead singer introduced everyone to the crowd, Lydia and Warren turned their attention to the stage. When introduced, Malcolm tossed his drumsticks in the air, deftly catching them again.

"Not sketchy, I guess. Just a show off." Warren met Lydia's eyes and touched her arm. "Are you almost done your shift?"

"Just a couple more hours to finish up. I'm not required to stay the whole evening."

"Me neither. See you later." Warren headed toward the closest door.

"Yeah, okay," she called, talking to his back.

He turned around, his smile accompanied by a thumbs up.

Lydia returned to work, smiling, too.

WARREN COULDN'T WAIT for this shift to end. He hadn't seen Lydia in four days, but somehow it seemed longer. Briefly talking to her after he spotted her talking to that guy in the band, had been a pleasure. And a worry also. Exactly how good of a friend was the guy? Would they renew their acquaintance or was the band passing through the city, perhaps on a tour? Hopefully, the latter.

Warren hung his chef's coat in his locker and grabbed the pale gray sportscoat he'd worn to work, hoping to run into Lydia. Hoping she'd agree to coffee? A first date of sorts. He'd brushed his teeth, gargled, combed his hair after removing his chef's hat. Done everything but pray to the first-date gods that she'd say yes when he suggested they go somewhere now that their shifts were ending. He'd better hustle or she'd give up waiting and leave for home!

Warren exited the BMO building and discovered Lydia leaning against the exterior wall. She wore white jeans and a black t-shirt with charcoal sandals. She'd removed her long strands of chestnut perfection from the bun she'd worn while working. Her eyes appeared to light up when she spotted him. Was she equally eager for them to spend time together?

"Hi! Am I late?"

"Not at all. I stepped outside a minute ago." Her smile broadened. "Between all the wedding guests talking at once, the sound of dishes rattling, and now the band playing, I needed some peace and quiet."

Warren laughed. "I know what you mean. Preparing that wedding meal was something else. Enough chaos for one day."

"You mentioned seeing me later." She winked. "It's later. What did you have in mind?"

He reached for her hand, pulling her away from the wall and drawing her into an embrace. "A beer somewhere or a coffee at Tim Hortons. Your choice."

"Coffee!" she exclaimed. "I couldn't handle a noisy bar."

"Tim's it is, gorgeous lady." Warren searched her eyes. Man, she was more beautiful every time he laid eyes on her.

She smiled at him and wrapped her arms around his neck. "A large mocha latte for me, please."

"Whatever your heart desires." He stood, staring into her eyes for a moment.

She slowly closed her eyes and that was his undoing. He closed his eyes and kissed her lips, holding her close, hoping she desired him as much as the fancy coffee she requested. She snuggled against him, and the light floral scent of her perfume reached his nose. Had he died and gone to heaven? He never wanted this kiss to end.

Just then the door opened and someone stepped outside. "Get a room."

Warren and Lydia broke their kiss and glanced over at the intruder. Warren visualized his boss standing there, and he suspected Lydia was doing the same. Instead, there stood Nick Jackson, grinning.

"Jealous much?" Warren accused, his arm reaching out and circling Lydia's waist.

Nick ignored Warren's question. "Hi, Lydia. You're looking as beautiful as ever."

"Th… thank you," she stammered, looking into Warren's eyes.

"Ignore him," he whispered, hearing Nick calling a farewell in the background.

Lydia giggled. "I'll try my best. Shouldn't be too difficult."

~

WARREN FOLLOWED Lydia to her apartment where she left her SUV in her designated parking spot. They took Warren's pickup to the nearest Tim Hortons and opted to order inside. Soon, they shared a table by the far window, the quietest spot in the restaurant right now.

"So, another week and Stampede will be well underway." Warren sipped his black coffee. None of that fancy stuff for him.

Lydia groaned. "Don't remind me. I have so much to do, to keep track of. I'm close to dreading Stampede this year."

"Come on, it can't be that bad."

Lydia grabbed her cell phone, opened the planner page for July, and passed him the phone.

"Holy crap!" Warren almost dropped it. "Every date has three or four things listed."

"Tell me about it!" She dropped her head into her hands. "And I'm praying I haven't forgotten anything."

"How did you get yourself into all this?" He passed her phone to her.

She stuffed it into the outside pocket on her oversized straw purse. "Except for participating in the Stampede Parade and the plans I made with my roommate, Emily, my mother volunteered me for most of it." She took a sip of her latte.

"Say no more." Warren nodded, vigorously. "My mother has been known to do the same to me and my brother. Signed us up for baseball or soccer or 4-H club. For our own good."

"Always for our own good." Lydia laughed, leaning back in her seat. "I'm certain Mom means well, but there are still only twenty-four hours in a day."

"Good luck, but I'm sure you'll be fine." Warren reached across the table and took her hand in his, massaging her palm with his thumb. Her hands were as soft as a kitten, surprising him considering how often a server had her hands in water.

"Thank you. I'll survive. Thank goodness it's only for ten days," she reasoned. "So, are you looking forward to Stampede?"

"Oh, yeah. It's going to be nuts. I couldn't be more excited. Nick has worked for Stampede before, and he's warned me about the long hours and hectic schedules and total chaos at times." He shifted forward in his seat. "Total pandemonium is probably the best training I could receive, in preparation for a position in a busy hotel kitchen some day."

Lydia gazed out the window. Warren followed her line of sight; the parking lot lit by street light was all he could see. Warren wondered about Lydia's plans for her own 'some day'. Wasn't she training as a nurse? "Is something else bothering you?"

She shook her head, and a yawn escaped her lips. "Nothing I want to get into tonight." She met his eyes, dark circles evident beneath hers.

"You look beat. Want me to take you home?"

"Yes, I'm so tired I could lay my head down on this table and fall asleep."

Warren stood and reached out a hand to her. "Come with me. Can't have you doing that. I'll have you home in no time."

Ten minutes later, he wrapped her in his arms as they stood, waiting for the elevator in her apartment building. "Sleep in tomorrow, if you're able to. You'll need all the sleep you can get before Stampede starts."

"Don't I know it."

They rode the elevator to her floor. She rose onto her tiptoes outside her suite and kissed him, surprising him by taking the lead.

Or was she hoping to send him on his way sooner? She turned the key in the lock and opened the door.

Warren took the hint and waited until she entered. "Goodnight," he whispered, touching her cheek as she lingered in the open doorway.

"Goodnight," she replied. "Why are we whispering?"

"You mentioned a roommate. Emily?"

"That's right, I did. I'm so tired, I forgot." Lydia shook her head. "Emily sleeps like the dead. A freight train could pass through the apartment and it wouldn't wake her up."

Warren laughed. "Oh. Okay. Good to know. Goodnight," he repeated in his normal tone of voice, and leaned forward, kissing her again.

"Goodnight. I hope to see you once Stampede starts."

"You will." He winked at her and headed down the hallway, hearing her apartment door closing. "I can guarantee it, pretty woman," he said, completing his thought.

When he climbed into his pickup, he caught himself humming the tune.

# CHAPTER 4

First Friday in July
Day one of Stampede

*L*ydia smiled, delighted to be part of the reason for the excitement in the air. She gaped in awe as she wandered around the meeting area where participants gathered and eventually were queued. Float judging had been completed hours ago and now everyone anticipated the beginning of the parade. So many businesses and organizations had entered floats, competing for the various prizes offered. With all these imaginative designs, she was thankful she hadn't been judging.

Members of a local horse club stood about while their horses tugged on the reins with hooves dancing in anticipation. She loved the beautiful animals which had played such an important role in Alberta's history, aiding ranchers and homesteaders and First Nations people, as well. Moving along, she spotted two Clydesdales hitched to a float, appearing a little bored. These two-thousand-pound horses were huge in comparison to the saddle horses her cousins raised. Lydia loved watching the beautiful creatures walking the parade route, lifting their feathered feet in their special way. A crowd pleaser for sure.

Much further away from the horses, she discovered a marching band, the musicians creating an ungodly cacophony as they tuned their individual instruments. In the distance, she heard bagpipes which were always popular with the crowd.

Craning her neck, she recognized several politicians and local dignitaries seated in open-air vehicles. One of the convertibles had been donated by a local dealership. Soon, they'd be waving to the crowd in hopes of creating goodwill and winning themselves votes for re-election. Calgary's popular mayor always rode a horse in the parade, but she hadn't seen him yet.

Several members of the RCMP walked on past her, dressed in their red tunics, breeches with the yellow stripe running down each side, tall boots polished to a sheen and distinctive Stetsons on their heads. The officers representing the famous Canadian police force always created an impressive sight, steps perfectly matched as they marched in practiced unison along the parade route.

Returning to the Tsuut'ina float and participants, she smiled at the familiar elders, including her grandfather, Bernard Crowchild, who waved to her from atop her cousin Ernest's horse. The horse-drawn float where drummers and dancers would ride, including her, stood behind the elders. Nerves niggled her mind and cued the butterflies to start dancing in her stomach. Every street along the Stampede Parade route would be filled with onlookers. She should be accustomed to this, having participated in the parade several years now.

She'd be fine once they got underway. One of her male cousins, a hoop dancer, helped her onto the float. Later, their float would stop completely and she would be helped down again to perform the shawl dance as they moved along the parade route.

Finally, parade organizers waved the Tsuut'ina riders and float forward to follow behind a beautifully decorated corporate float featuring representatives waving to the crowds, free of music or noise so as not to startle the horses, as was Stampede policy. It probably wouldn't matter though, her cousin's experienced horses were accustomed to the loud drumming. Lydia would have to inquire if the corporation had won a prize.

From the sidewalks, children shouted and waved to the people passing by on the parade floats. A dull murmur rumbled throughout the crowd. Thousands of spectators would be seated on lawn chairs on the sidewalks, coolers with snacks and cold drinks nearby. People settled in to watch, as many as four or five deep. The back row of onlookers leaned on storefronts, hoping for a clear view.

Clowns wandered along the parade route, entertaining the crowd with their antics. Lydia recalled how terrified of the clowns she'd been as a child, wrapping her arms around her mother's leg and hiding her face in her clothing whenever one approached her. Now, one of her best friends was married to a rodeo clown, one of the people working to keep bull riders safe. Lydia considered him a special person, since there had to be an easier way to make a living!

Several Tsuut'tina members had been helped off the float, her among them. Now, Lydia danced proudly with her head held high, following behind the chief and elders. She recalled as a child being proud of her heritage, seeing her people representing the Tsuut'ina nation as she watched and cheered with her parents from the sidelines. Then years later, participating in the parade herself and still hoping to continue the tradition for years to come.

Drummers sang to the familiar beat as they rode along on the decorated float behind the dancers. Lydia relished the feeling of freedom of expression she experienced whenever she performed the fancy shawl dance. From years of training and competition, her feet moved at will without her having to think about the dance steps. This sparkling aqua blue and spring grass-colored dress was one of her favorites, and she'd won several dancing competitions at powwows while wearing it. As she performed the dance, mimicking a butterfly in flight, her heart swelled with pride and she couldn't be happier. Without any breeze today, she was sweating slightly inside her costume. The drumming increased in volume, louder, louder still. Right on cue, her feet stopped with the final beat of the drum. In competition, a dancer would lose points otherwise. Chest heaving and slightly out of breath, Lydia waved to the crowd. The onlookers' applause spoke of their appreciation.

The drumming resumed and she glanced to her right where her favorite cousin, Ernest, and several other young men performed the hoop dance, wearing their most colorful, feathered costumes. Ernest's arms formed wings with the multitude of hoops, his arms mimicking a bird in flight as part of the dance. And with one quick movement he, along with the others, created a circle with the hoops representing the world. Ernest's talent amazed her, and he'd won countless competitions to prove it. Several Tsuut'ina members were dancing today. All of them were competitors in hoop dance, war dance, fancy dance and shawl dance. Lydia and the others continued down the street, amid enthusiastic applause from the crowd.

Lydia loved being in this parade every year, but she worried how many more times she'd be able to participate if she decided on a nursing career. Would work schedules interfere with parade days? She wouldn't be able to ignore the needs of the sick, whether working on the reserve or in a city hospital. If she finished her training. She wouldn't worry about it now. Not when she was having so much fun.

"Yahoo!" several onlookers shouted from the sidelines.

Lydia smiled at the crowd, doing what she loved. Her mother, Melanie Simpson-Crowchild, had entered her in that first dance competition when she was ten years old after several months of lessons. Her mother and father had cheered her on from the sidelines. Wearing her jingle dress and having little idea of what was happening, she recalled being devastated that she hadn't won a prize. But she'd immediately been hooked. She'd grown to love competing and dancing, honoring her First Nations heritage. Now, she'd lost count of the number of prizes she'd won.

Years ago, her Caucasian father had encouraged her love of dancing and cheered her on as loudly as her First Nations relatives. An oilfield accident ended Samuel Simpson's life, the summer she turned sixteen. She missed seeing him smiling, waving, and cheering when she competed. He'd left a substantial life insurance policy and she and her mother would never want for anything. But she'd forfeit every penny of her monthly allowance to still have her father in her life.

Lydia hadn't been paying attention to the blur of faces in the crowd, intent on her performance. Emily would be here somewhere along the route; her university roomie had the day off. And several relatives and other members of the Tsuut'ina nation would be cheering from the sidelines as well. Had Warren arranged time off to attend?

The float with the Western band and singers followed a-ways behind them so as not to frighten their horses, but Lydia recognized the lyrics to the Blake Shelton tune they were playing. She glanced back and noticed several people in the crowd were singing along while the float passed by them. She laughed aloud when a middle-aged couple clambered off their lawn chairs and began dancing a two-step on the sidelines, encouraged by cheers from the crowd.

"Yahoo!" shouted another onlooker. She'd hear it dozens of times today.

Lydia faced forward again. Photographers from a variety of media outlets roamed the sidelines of the parade route, looking for a front-page-worthy shot. One of them, a man with a bushy mop of blond hair and a trim mustache, had taken a close-up of her, smiling with her shawl fully extended. She'd faint if that picture made the local papers!

But the Calgary Stampede was all about the fascinating history of Alberta and the famous Western hospitality still alive today. On second thought, having her picture associated with this fine tradition wouldn't be bad at all.

~

WARREN COULDN'T CONTAIN his excitement. The first day of Stampede meant the start to a steady stream of events and catering and supplying food requirements for most every Stampede venue on the grounds, except the midway. Thinking about it had him smiling.

"Hey, break time, buddy," Nick Jackson called on his way to the break room. "The parade is being televised. We should check it out."

Warren set his chef knife down and wiped his hands on a towel. "Be right there."

When Warren entered the break room, Nick handed him a cup of coffee. They settled onto the upholstered chairs and gazed up at the flat screen TV hanging on the wall. Someone had flipped it onto the channel broadcasting live coverage of the Stampede Parade.

"I haven't seen the parade in person in years."

Warren chuckled. "Me neither. Always working."

"At least we can catch a few minutes of it." Nick parked his feet on another chair and sipped his coffee.

Several floats passed by on the screen, mostly representing local businesses and corporations. A clown stepped up to the camera, making a nuisance of himself.

"Hey, she looks familiar." Nick pointed to the screen.

Warren nodded. With the camera zooming in on Lydia, he easily recognized her. "She works here as a server." He couldn't help admiring how gracefully Lydia moved, dancing in a blue-green dress. Man, she was beautiful. He straightened in his chair, mesmerized by her movements. Her moccasin-clad feet executed the dance steps, her arms extended to display her matching shawl to best advantage, the long multi-colored fringes in blues, pinks and orange tones swept through the air with her arms' movements, soaring and dipping. Two tidy braids lay on her shoulders, two feathers extended out from a butterfly clamp at the back of her head. Beaded earrings hung from her earlobes and she wore the broadest smile he'd ever seen. Her body twirled while her feet danced to the drum beat. Her excellent physical shape was evident; she maintained constant energetic enthusiasm the entire duration of the dance. Damn, he recalled her kisses and his body heated.

"She's representing one of the Seven Nations."

"The what?" Warren mumbled.

Nick glanced over at him. "The Treaty Seven Nations: the Blackfoot Confederacy, the Stoney Nakoda and the Tsuut'ina Nation, all in Southern Alberta."

Warren wondered which one Lydia was representing.

As if he'd read his co-worker's thoughts, Nick added, "Looks like she's part of the Tsuut'ina Nation."

"She's the server that nearly knocked me senseless the other night." Senseless in more ways than one. Warren couldn't get the beautiful woman or her kisses out of his mind.

"It was her? She's gorgeous. She can knock me over anytime," Nick muttered.

Warren glared at his friend. "Her boss didn't fire her, though I know he heard about it. She must be a damn good server."

"Must be."

"I've seen her working the premium venues like ranahans and weddings at The Lazy S and the Palomino Ballroom," Warren added.

Nick shook his head. "Why haven't I ever noticed her?"

Warren burst out laughing. "You're too busy chasing blue-eyed blondes."

"Hey!" Nick started to object and then shrugged his shoulders. "Fair enough. But I guess it's obvious you prefer brown-eyed beauties like her."

Warren's collar on his chef coat had become a little too tight. "Yeah, I've noticed her. What guy wouldn't? But I've got my eye on my goal. Becoming an executive chef is too important to be side-tracked by a woman, no matter how beautiful she is."

"Well, if you're not interested, maybe I've been wasting my time on those blondes. I should consider dating that brown-eyed beauty."

"Don't even think about it," Warren blurted. Now, why the hell had he said that? He'd never been plagued by the green-eyed monster, as his mother would say. He could only describe Lydia as nothing more than an acquaintance. He couldn't say whether or not she'd forgiven him for his reprimand the other night. His superiors hadn't questioned him about the incident, and no one had fired her. Perhaps everyone considered it an unfortunate accident, a lesson learned, and left it at that.

"Eye on your goal?" Nick scoffed. "Yeah, right. If you're making a choice between strictly concentrating on your career or that gorgeous Indigenous woman, my money is on her."

Warren set his coffee mug down. "Time to get back to work." He strode out of the break room. Why did he warn Nick away from Lydia? Sure, an attraction between them existed. But did he want her for himself? He returned to his work station, sharpening his chef's knife again before resuming his work, prepping root vegetables.

Nick could wager all he wanted. Warren had his heart set on applying for the executive chef position he'd dreamed of holding for years. He would love seeing Nick lose his shirt in a wager.

But that would mean Warren would have to keep his eyes and attention off Lydia. When the opportunity presented itself the other night in the parking lot, he shouldn't have kissed her. Twenty-twenty hindsight. He hoped Nick was the man doing the losing. Because Warren worried he could quite easily be losing his heart to her. He couldn't let that happen. Not yet anyway. Reaching his goal was too important.

# CHAPTER 5

Saturday
Day two of Stampede

Knowing her cousin's baby shower wouldn't end until ten p.m. or later, Lydia stayed over at her mother's house last night. Up, showered and dressed, Lydia wandered down the hallway from her bedroom and entered the kitchen. Her mother sat at the round oak table, drinking a cup of coffee, dressed in dark jeans, a white cotton top and black sandals. Slim and fit, with very few grays in her shoulder-length black hair, her mother could pass for mid-thirties instead of forty-seven. Strangers occasionally mistook them for sisters.

"*Guja nagudigoy.*" Melanie Simpson-Crowchild smiled at her daughter.

"Good morning," Lydia echoed her mother's greeting. "You're still here?"

"I could ask you the same?"

"I'm leaving as soon as I make a cup of coffee." Lydia strode across the tile floor to the Keurig and popped a pod inside. She set her favorite happy-face mug on the stand and pushed START.

Lydia stared out the kitchen window. Was this the right time to bring up the most troubling concern on her mind these days? After her father died so young, she'd felt honor bound to follow his footsteps into the corporate world. For several years after high school, she'd worked as an executive assistant in an oilfield company. But she'd never felt at home in the business industry. She'd hated it! Uncomfortable in her father's corporate world, she'd decided one day she required a new career.

Her mother worked for years in community health and home care in the Community Health Centre on the Tsuut'ina reserve, and Lydia wanted to help people also. She recalled many times when she was a little girl, playing hospital with her mom. Bandaging her dolls and teddy bears, listening for imaginary heartbeats with a plastic stethoscope. She smiled at the memories of saving those inanimate lives. Following in her mother's footsteps and becoming a registered nurse had seemed the logical path to take.

Nursing was probably the career she should have chosen years ago, and perhaps would have had her father not died. She'd finally been accepted at the University of Calgary and began her training three years ago. Years one and two centered on theory, and she'd loved it. But considering the horrendous third year she'd completed —interacting with patients seemed her downfall—she'd been harboring innumerable doubts whether getting her nursing degree had been the right decision.

But how would Lydia explain her worries and fears to her mother who loved her own career in nursing? How would Lydia explain, or ever attempt to justify, three years of wasted time and money? Lydia couldn't face the possibility of once again disappointing the person who loved her the most. The entire situation was impossible. She couldn't face continuing; she couldn't handle quitting.

"Where are you working this morning?"

"You mean you don't know? You're the reason I'm going," Lydia grumbled, leaning against the counter. Actually, she was helping the elders and then serving at a Stampede event later tonight. But why bother bringing up her mother's interference in her life again? The two of them were never going to agree on this.

"Your grandfather mentioned you were unhappy." Her mother set her coffee mug on the table and shoved it aside.

"Mom, I'm furious! My cell phone is crammed full of scheduled events. I'm trying desperately to keep track of all the things you volunteered me for. Helping the elders at storytelling, and the vendors with their craft sales. Working in the Bannock Booth. Not to mention my shifts at Stampede Catering."

Melanie met her daughter's eyes. "Oh, my girl. What do people think of when they hear the word 'Stampede'?"

Lydia shrugged her shoulders. "Cowboys and bucking broncos, and chuckwagon drivers racing their rigs around the half mile of Hell."

"Exactly."

"Is there a point to your question?"

"Cowboys. Bull riders. Men. What about the women of Stampede?"

"The women?" Lydia had to admit her mother had piqued her interest.

"Stampede is more than cowboys. What about the wives, girl-friends, mothers and sisters who assist with caring for the horses? Helping out in the barns? Preparing meals and accomplishing a hundred different things behind the scenes for their families? What about the women who compete in barrel-racing?"

Lydia shook her head. "Okay. Ranch people. What does that have to do with me?"

"There are the women who enter their baking, sewing, crafts and paintings in the various contests. And consider the hundreds of women who volunteer for Stampede. First Nations women who work at the Indian Village, selling their handcrafts or volunteering at the Bannock Booth. Don't forget the women and young girls who sing and entertain as part of the Grandstand Show every night."

Lydia nodded, conceding her mother had a point.

Her mother continued, "The women of Stampede make an invaluable contribution during those ten days, as well as before and after. Some all year long."

"I know where you're going with this," Lydia hedged. "You're enticing me to continue your legacy as a Stampede worker and volunteer."

"Is that such a bad thing?" Her mother playfully tugged on the long braid hanging over Lydia's right shoulder.

"Not at all. I love Stampede," Lydia admitted. "First Nations people have participated in the festivities since 1912 when Guy Weadick started the whole thing. He insisted native peoples be a part of the celebration. But I'd like some free time to spend with my friends, and I'd like to choose where to offer my time and talents. And most importantly, Mom, doing it in moderation."

"Next year, I will leave the decisions to you." Her mother patted her arm. "But please continue to work at Indian Village and show pride in your heritage."

"I always will, Mom. I promise." Lydia hugged her mother tightly.

"That's all I ask." Her mom smiled at her. "And my beautiful daughter, by volunteering at the Indian Village and serving at Stampede Catering, you already are a Woman of Stampede."

Lydia smiled and poured her coffee into a travel mug. "Thanks, Mom. But please remember, you can't volunteer me anymore this year! Emily wants to do the midway a couple nights during the week, and I haven't a spare moment to think straight."

"Emily's parents are wealthy. She has nothing better to do than go to the midway and spend her money shopping all day. Emily can afford to waste away her summer."

Lydia snorted, in a rather unladylike way. "Let me remind you that Dad left us a half million dollars from his life insurance policy.

His money manager's talent with high interest investments constantly increases the original principle, and with the monthly allowances we both receive, neither of us needs to work."

Her mother nodded, acknowledging Lydia had a point. "But we do work, so we can buy a new SUV when we need one," her mother stated, reminding Lydia of the recent purchase of her lease-return vehicle. "And wear nice clothes, and enjoy a vacation every winter. Mostly, we love keeping busy, you and I. We want to make a difference in this world. We want to help others."

"I know. I know. That's why you're a nurse here on the reserve." Lydia shifted to her other foot. "Just because people have money, no matter their race, doesn't mean they're lazy or waste their time. Emily works part-time at the Chinook Mall and she volunteers once a week at a hospital."

"I didn't know that. Good for Emily." Her mother set her coffee mug on the counter and approached Lydia, hugging her tightly. "She's a better friend for you than I thought, and I'm sorry for making incorrect assumptions about her. It is good that you defended Emily. Hold your best friends close to your heart."

Lydia closed her eyes, relishing her mother's warm embrace and kind words. Lydia didn't have many friends, and Emily was special to her. The sister she would never have. Since the day her father died when she was only sixteen, Lydia and her mother had faced life alone. Her mother had never remarried, seldom dated. In many ways, she'd been Lydia's best friend for the past ten years. "Speaking of friends. Last November, Emily and I bought tickets when they first went on sale for the Luke Bryan concert on Saturday night. You *cannot* volunteer me for anything that night. I am *not* missing this concert."

"Of course not. When people work hard, they deserve a little fun. I love his music but I couldn't get tickets. All sold out. So enjoy the concert for both of us." Her mother smiled.

"Yes, I do work hard," Lydia agreed, glancing at her cell phone. "Oh, no. I'm going to be late!" Already dressed for work, she grabbed her purse from the countertop. She hoped she'd see Warren Chamberland again tonight, if he was working the same event as her. Despite her best efforts, she couldn't get the handsome chef out of her mind. But she wasn't ready to share news of her attraction to him with her mother.

"Drive safely. Traffic in the city is crazy with all the tourists here for Stampede. Avoid rush hour if possible," her mom warned.

"I will."

"I have to hurry myself. I'm helping at the Bannock Booth today." Melanie reached for her car keys hanging on the peg by the door. "Lydia, my girl, I'm very proud of the wonderful young woman you've grown up to be. And someday you'll make a difference in many, many lives when you graduate as a nurse."

"Tonight's corporate event shouldn't run too late. Emily works until ten, so I don't have plans for tonight. I should be home shortly after nine," Lydia called as she headed out the door.

*Make a difference.*

Lydia cringed, recalling her mother's words, as she climbed into her SUV. Don't be too sure, Mom. I'm not, especially with the becoming-a-nurse thing still up in the air. How does a person know when they've found their purpose in life? She hadn't a clue, but she'd better discover the answer soon.

# CHAPTER 6

*L*ydia lounged at a picnic table provided by one of the midway's refreshment booths, sipping an iced tea, surrounded by bustling activity. Children were laughing and babies crying, adults attempting to keep track of their children amid all the chaos associated with the midway on a pleasant-weather day. The afternoon sun beat down, warming and soothing her from head to toe. She spent so many hours working indoors that being outside felt wonderful.

She watched a young couple maneuvering their way through the crowd with four pre-school children in tow. Definitely outnumbered by that gang. "Thank goodness I don't have kids yet," she muttered.

She gazed upward, allowing the sun to warm her face. One fluffy white cloud floated low in the otherwise clear blue sky, the air humid today after last night's rain showers. There wasn't a hint of breeze to cool her off. The scent of greasy carnival food hung in the air and assaulted her nose.

She grabbed her phone and opened her email for any new items her mother may have added to her schedule. Thankfully, she hadn't any extra catering commitments, and so far, her duties at the Indian

Village had become manageable with only a couple of changes. A damn miracle considering her mother's interference in her life. Stampede was such a fun time, but being double-booked and letting someone down was her greatest worry during these ten days of insanity.

Lydia checked the time. *One o'clock.* Hopefully, Malcolm wouldn't be much longer, but he'd never been the punctual type. She set her cell on the table and sipped her iced tea. Light and refreshing, and what she needed after her morning shift at the Bannock Booth.

Seated at a nearby table, a young couple gazed into each other's eyes. They were completely oblivious to everyone else, including Lydia who caught herself smiling. New love? Summer love? True love? Did they realize how lucky they were to have found each other?

Lydia turned away, the picture they made a little too painful. She'd been so preoccupied with school, and now her Stampede schedule, that dating hadn't crossed her mind. But then she'd met Warren Chamberland, aka hunky sous chef. Why couldn't she get him off of her mind? Instead, every night before falling asleep images of him stole their way into her thoughts. And later into her dreams. She warmed all over recalling last night's sexy episode conjured up by her subconscious self.

Lydia sipped her iced tea, but soon her thoughts returned to the handsome chef, the first man she'd felt a strong, immediate attraction to in ages. And now that she'd met him, she secretly hoped their acquaintanceship eventually might turn into more. But would her mother approve of her getting involved with Warren? With any guy? Was her mother keeping her busy, hoping she would enjoy dancing all summer and then concentrate on her studies come autumn?

"Does Mom not want me involved with anyone, even for a few innocent dates?" Lydia speculated, muttering aloud.

"Hey, you talking to yourself?"

The familiar male voice sent Lydia's heartbeat racing. She swung around on the bench seat, feeling her face redden. "No! I am not talking to myself," she argued, knowing full well that's exactly what she'd been doing. "Whether justified or not, people who talk to themselves are considered crazy."

"Well then, pardon me. I must be mistaken. Although I heard it was a sign of genius." Warren winked at her, slipping into the seat opposite her on the picnic table.

Lydia's heartbeat raced when he winked at her, showing his playful side.

"I noticed you in the parade yesterday. You looked great in that green-blue dress and the other part with the colorful fringes." Warren smiled warmly, settling onto the bench seat. "And you danced beautifully."

She caught herself grinning. "Thank you. The shawl dance mimics a butterfly in flight."

"Really? You learn something new all the time." Warren tilted his head. "Yeah, I get that. The way your arms moved."

"It's my favorite dance. I compete at powwows every summer, including these next two months. And I loved performing in the parade."

"I could tell. I watched part of it on the TV during my break at work. But you were smiling the entire time I got to watch." He gazed into her eyes. "You have a great smile."

Lydia couldn't think of a response. Did she appear as stunned as she felt?

Warren leaned forward. "So what were you *not* talking to yourself about?"

"Nothing important," she muttered, reality crashing around her.

Warren pointed to her cardboard cup. "Want another one of those? I'm so thirsty I could drink dishwater."

Lydia smiled. "It's hot today! That would be nice, thank you. Iced tea, not the dishwater."

Warren laughed. "Glad you clarified that. Iced tea it is." He leapt off the bench, returning a couple minutes later with two large iced teas. He handed one to Lydia and for a brief moment their hands touched, sending an electric current rushing up her arm and warming her entire body. As if she needed the extra heat today!

"Thank you." Her voice sounded a little breathy. She took a sip to cool herself down a bit. Why did this man have such an explosive effect on her? Whether a simple smile or a sly wink, he sent her emotions into orbit.

"What's up? Are you scheduled to serve at an event or work anywhere?"

"Not right now. I worked at the Indian Village in the Bannock Booth. I have the rest of the afternoon free." She sipped her iced tea. For some reason, her temperature kept rising, the longer they talked. Listening to his deep, sexy voice mesmerized her. Why was he so darn handsome?

When she recalled the initial reason she'd wanted this time to think, she heaved a sigh before she could stop herself.

Warren reached out and gently took her hand in his. "Is something wrong?"

She shook her head.

He searched her eyes, no doubt looking for an answer to her emotions. "Talk to me. What has you upset?"

"My life is a mess." Now why had she blurted that out?

"Sometimes when you're working, I've noticed your thoughts seem a million miles away." Warren sipped his iced tea.

"Remember I told you about my mother volunteering me for so many things. Thankfully, no conflicts occurred with my catering shifts so far. But I keep waiting for something to come to light that will mess up my schedule. I've spoken with Mom, but I'm not certain it'll do any good."

"Well, a bit of advice." Warren reached for her hand, offering comfort again. "Set your priorities and then stick to them. Insist your mother respect your time and learn to say 'no' when she crosses any lines."

Lydia heaved another sigh. "I've done that. And I've insisted that I want time with my friends, too."

"Time for dating me?" Warren grinned.

Lydia smiled. "Yes, but saying no to my mother is like telling the sun to stop rising every morning." She took another sip and then cradled her cup in her hands. "But I think we're coming to an understanding."

"I went through a situation with my father, years ago," Warren confessed. "I grew up on a cattle ranch west of High River, and my father assumed I'd graduate high school and then attend university. Dad figured like my brother, Blaine, I'd get a degree in agriculture, then take over the ranch some day with my brother when he decided to retire."

Lydia leaned forward in her seat. "But you had other ideas?"

"Skipped university after graduating from high school. Just worked on the ranch for far too many years. When I'd finally had enough, I told my family I was training to become a chef, with the goal of becoming one of Canada's best." Warren shook his head. "I thought the roof would come off the house that morning over breakfast, but my dad surprised me. I think he'd figured out I hated ranching."

"He'd been waiting for you to announce what you wanted to do in life?" she speculated.

"My father is a rancher, only a high school graduate. But he's pretty wise, and he gave me some sound advice." Warren paused to finish his iced tea and then set the cup aside. "I'm going to share his advice with you."

"Please do. I need all the help I can get. I'm not only concerned with my Stampede schedule. I have my nursing career to consider also."

Warren took a deep breath. "Dad told me, *saddle a dream and then ride it to completion.*"

Lydia gaped at him. "Saddle a dream? I can't even saddle a horse."

Warren burst out laughing.

"I'm serious. Stop laughing at me."

He held up his hands. "Okay. I'm sorry. But if you want to rely on luck, visit a casino. If you want to achieve a dream or reach a goal, then get busy. It'll only happen with proper training, hard work and determination. Put your heart into it or get out."

"That's what I'm trying to decide, now that I completed my third year of nurse's training."

Warren shifted on the bench seat. "Well, call me crazy, but doesn't that mean you intend to become a nurse?"

"Yeah, I'd considered it. But I spent too much time in tears last year. I cried every time I saw sick kids, old people die, accident victims, people requiring surgeries, newborn babies. Damn near everything." She felt herself blushing.

"I hear the frustration in your voice. And how much this is troubling you." Warren moved around to the other side of the picnic table and wrapped his arm around Lydia.

She shifted sideways and his arm slid off her shoulder. "Don't do that, please, or I'll embarrass myself with tears," she whispered.

"So you think you're too soft hearted?"

"Exactly."

"And that's the only reason? Or are you getting failing marks?" One of his eyebrows rose.

"I'm an honor student. Straight As. 3.9 GPA."

"Those marks tell me you're definitely meant to be a nurse."

"I don't think so."

Warren leaned over and kissed her lips. He looked into her eyes, concern evident on his face. "Then saddle another dream. One you're certain you're intended to pursue. And then go for it."

"You make it sound so simple." Lydia shook her head, knowing he genuinely wanted to help her sort out her situation. And she couldn't be more appreciative. He represented an uninvolved third party with a totally unprejudiced opinion, someone who could see the issue from all sides without any preconceived insights. If he'd only stop kissing her, perhaps she could think more clearly. "What about tuition? Education costs a lot of money."

"You're talking about the rest of your life. Student loans can be repaid. You have your entire life's work to consider here. Nobody should be saddled with a job they hate." Warren grinned. "Sorry about the pun."

"Actually, my father died when I was sixteen. His life insurance left a ton of money for my education. That isn't the issue. I hate wasting money on things that will never come to fruition. Not to mention, I'm twenty-five and have no idea what I should be when I grow up." She smiled at him.

"Well, you're definitely grown up. Whatever you decide to do, go for it. Make it happen." Warren gently squeezed her hand. "I wasted a lot of time on the family ranch. Then I decided I was becoming an executive chef. Now at age thirty, my goal is finally in sight. I've put in the hours and I aced the Red Seal exam last year before I was hired by Stampede. After this summer, I'm sending out my resume to high-end hotels."

"High-end hotels?"

"My dream job is executive chef at the Fairmont Palliser downtown." Warren tapped the table with his fingers. "I'm going to land that job or die trying. Or at least find a similar position. I've set my sights on my dream and absolutely *nothing* is going to stop me. Nothing!"

Lydia paused in her response. He sounded so self-assured about his future, conviction bordering on arrogance. *Nothing?* Tell that to a football player who had sustained one concussion too many. Or a hockey player who became a paraplegic after a vehicular accident. Or a professional bull rider who broke his spine when trampled during a fall.

She gazed into Warren's eyes. If only she could muster up half of his passion. "I'm so tired of trying to find my dream. I felt I had, but I'm not certain I'm emotionally strong enough for nursing. Maybe I should quit now and cut my losses."

"You're stronger than you think. Even emotionally. You stood up to me when I reprimanded you in June. I think you might make a wonderful nurse." He dragged his fingers through the facial hair on his chin, a habit she'd noticed before.

She gazed at him. She loved running her fingers through his wavy brown hair when they kissed. And her stomach did crazy flipflops whenever she looked into his eyes. Such a nice man, and he wasn't prejudiced against other races, showing so much interest in her and her problems. He sounded like he believed in her, more than she did herself.

"Thank you for listening and for your encouragement." Lydia smiled. She had two months to decide if she should return to school. Worst case scenario, she'd have to tell her mother she'd wasted another three years of time and money, without any idea where she was headed in life.

"Happy to help." Warren stood, preparing to leave.

Lydia smiled, climbing over the bench seat in hopes of getting a kiss goodbye. He smiled when she reached up and her fingers touched his cheek; his neatly trimmed beard always so soft.

He clasped her hand and raised it to his lips, kissing each finger. One at a time. She rose up on her tiptoes and smiled. He stared into her eyes and she gazed into his.

"Hey, Lydia!"

She turned and waved, having totally forgotten the other reason she was there. "I've been waiting for him," she admitted, glancing at Warren as Malcolm Jack approached the picnic table.

"Isn't he the drummer we saw at the Monroe wedding last Saturday?" He frowned as he spoke.

Lydia nodded, glancing at her cell phone. "Malcolm, you're an hour late! If Warren hadn't happened along, I would have left long ago. What's with you anyway?"

"Sorry." He grinned. "I'm usually waking up about now."

Lydia shook her head and met Warren's eyes. "We're going to Ranchman's on Macleod Trail for a beer and a bite to eat. Get caught up on each other's news, before I have to work later today at five o'clock."

"And I want to check out the mechanical bull. See if I can stay on longer than my usual three seconds," Malcolm added, laughing.

"You were better than that." Lydia touched his arm. "Almost made eight seconds a few times."

Malcolm nodded. "But it's a bunch of metal and leather, not a real bull remember."

"So, you're on a date together," Warren muttered.

Lydia shrugged. "I wouldn't call a bite to eat with a friend a date."

"No, man, not a date. But I'm hoping I can convince her to come on the road with us for a while. See some of the country. Have some fun." Malcolm settled his arm around Lydia's shoulders, smiling broadly. "Have you ever heard this woman sing? We sang together in high school. She'd be a great addition to our band. Can you think of a better way to spend the summer?"

Lydia's mouth dropped open and Warren appeared ready to strangle Malcolm for suggesting such a thing. Clearly, Warren didn't like the idea. She had to admit traveling with a country band was the farthest thing from her mind. Why had Malcolm come up with the idea? And what would make him think she'd ever accept his invitation?

Singing in a band and forgoing the opportunity to complete her nurse's training?

She looked heavenward. Really?

"Lydia didn't tell you she's in nurse's training?" Warren blurted. "Earning a degree to become an RN?"

Lydia shifted, slipping out from under Malcolm's arm. "It's true. I should be starting my final year in September. No singing aspirations here. I don't even sing in the church choir anymore."

"So come with us for the rest of the summer," Malcolm suggested.

Warren met her eyes. "Wouldn't that interfere with your plans for competitive dancing at powwows? You're really good."

Lydia smiled. He'd remembered everything she'd told him. And he sounded so passionate, defending the plans she'd made. Offering her an out by sprinkling a seed of reason into the conversation in contrast to Malcolm's spur-of-the-moment suggestion. Obviously, Warren considered Malcolm's offer of singing in a modestly successful band a poor substitute for a career in nursing.

Of course, he was right.

"Singing as a career has never been a dream of mine. Thanks for the offer, Malcolm, but no thanks!" Lydia laughed and slipped her arm through his. "However, I need to work at catering later. So let's hurry up and go for that beer and a burger anyway, and get caught up on each other's news."

"Whatever. Nice seeing you again, man." Malcolm waved as he steered Lydia away.

Lydia looked back. "Maybe I'll see you at work tonight," she called.

Warren stared at her. Was he a little jealous she'd made plans with another guy? He had nothing to worry about, but Lydia liked the idea he wasn't so certain of that.

CHAPTER 7

Sunday
Day Three of Stampede

*L*ydia gazed across the food court at the Chinook Shopping Mall, attempting to spot the person she was supposed to meet.

"Lydia!"

She heard the familiar voice calling her name and she whipped around. "Emily!" She waved and smiled, returning the greeting.

Seconds later, her friend hugged her tightly. "I can't believe you're here!"

"Of course, I'm here." Lydia laughed. "When I make a date I keep it. But I can't promise anything until the last minute since I never know what my mother will volunteer me for next."

"It's crazy what your mother did to you," Emily said, sympathizing.

Lydia nodded. "I know. But she means well. Mom has volunteered at Stampede for years and she has it in her head I should follow in her footsteps."

"Will you find time to come to the midway with me?" Emily crossed her fingers.

Lydia grasped her friend's arm. "I am not missing out on time together with you. We're going to the midway, but I can't say for certain when I'll be able to make it."

"Well, let's make plans to meet at the Stampede grounds on Tuesday night around nine o'clock. I'm done early at the mall." Emily linked arms with Lydia and steered her toward an empty table.

"Let me see." Lydia squeezed out of her friend's hold and checked her cell phone. "Yes! I don't work on Tuesday evening either. It's a date!"

Emily playfully wiped her brow. "Thank goodness."

They each bought a latte and searched for somewhere to sit. Emily spotted a vacant table at the far side and they wended their way between the tables. Lydia slid onto one of the four chairs, set her purse down, and smiled at the cowboy hat design the barista had added to her latte. Very appropriate for Stampede.

Lydia tipped her head, pointing at Emily. "Is this another new dress?"

"Yes. I love the discount at work, but it would be nice to get a full paycheck for a change." Emily laughed and took a seat across from her. "I also love the fact we're the same size. Can I wear those pink heels in your closet for my date tomorrow night?"

"Sure, no problem."

"Thanks, Lydia." Emily sipped her latte.

"Now, as long as Mom doesn't spring some surprise on me, we're good to go for Tuesday!" Lydia exclaimed.

"You need to stand up for yourself. Tell your mother to stop volunteering you for things without asking first."

"I know, Em. But I don't want Mom upset."

"Well, she has certainly been upsetting your life."

Lydia sighed. "But if I have to break the news I'm not returning to school in the fall, I don't want her angry with me already."

Emily's mouth dropped open. "Why on earth would you not return to nurse's training with me in the fall?"

Lydia looked away. She'd also been dreading this conversation with her roommate.

"Lydia, what's going on? Did something happen? Are you sick?" Emily touched her hand.

"Heavens, no! I'm simply not cut out to be a nurse." Lydia's shoulders slumped. There, she'd initiated the conversation, but she knew Emily wouldn't let her away with such a broad statement. Her friend would demand details, reasons, logic. And Lydia wasn't certain there was anything logical about her concerns.

Or was it simply fear? Fear of failing a patient who'd been depending on her? Life or death. She shivered, thinking about someone losing their life due to her emotional incompetence.

Emily leaned back in her chair, arms crossed. "Really? Miss A-student who aces all of her assignments and tests. Yeah, you haven't a clue what you're doing. You're totally failing at this nursing thing."

"Stop it. I'm serious." Lydia stared at her friend. How would she ever make Emily understand when she didn't fully comprehend her own reasoning?

Emily rolled her eyes. "Then explain it to me."

"I'm too soft-hearted. Too emotional. All I do is cry when I see an ill child, an old person on death's doorstep, an accident victim fighting for their life." Lydia's voice cracked.

"Oh, that."

"Yeah, that." Lydia blinked back tears. "See! I'm tearing up talking about this."

"Lots of the girls cry over those things." Emily sipped her latte. "Don't worry. The traumatic things we see will get easier with time."

"Not one other student has stood sobbing to the point they had to leave the patient's bedside." Lydia groaned, shaking her head. "I'm not so sure I'll ever overcome this."

"You will." Emily grasped both of Lydia's hands. "And you don't always have to leave. Plenty of times you've completed your work and then burst into tears in the hallway."

"My greatest fear is costing someone their life. Panicking in an emergency. Standing with tears streaming down my face, frozen in place, and someone taking their last breath because of me."

"Oh, Lydia." Emily leapt up, tugged her friend off her chair and wrapped her arms around her. "You're worried about this, aren't you?"

"Worried? Em, I'm terrified. I don't think I can return to school. I truly don't." Lydia brushed the wetness from her cheeks, feeling her face redden. "This is so embarrassing," she whispered, crying in the middle of the food court.

Emily settled into her chair and Lydia slumped onto her seat.

"Doing the right thing will become second nature in time." Emily touched Lydia's hand. "Another full year of university before our training is complete. Hours of practical training. You'll be a wonderful nurse. I know it."

Lydia forced a smile. "I wish I had your confidence. What if nothing ever becomes second nature? What if I've wasted all that time and money training to become an RN and then I suck at it?"

Emily laughed. "You won't suck at it."

"Can I get that in writing?" Lydia teased. "Maybe if I see it in print I'll believe it."

"Lydia, remember the time we returned from class and that little boy had fallen off his bike and scraped his knee and his wire-rimmed glasses cut his face above his eyebrow? You calmed him down and assured him he'd be okay while I buzzed his mother's apartment number and explained what happened?"

"Yeah, but he…"

"No but about it. You were wonderful with him, and you stopped the bleeding with a wad of tissues from your purse."

"His mom told us he required two stitches and she gave us the Tim Hortons gift card for coming to his rescue." Lydia smiled. It felt good to share her worries with another person, especially a good

friend like Emily. A fellow nursing student. If anyone would understand, Em should. And she'd reminded Lydia of their good deed.

"You'll graduate. And I'll be right beside you. We'll be two of
the best RNs ever," Emily stated.

Emily spoke her prediction with such conviction that Lydia
almost believed her. Should Lydia put her faith in herself, in the
training she'd receive? Would she become competent, efficient,
everything she'd dreamed of? She'd helped the boy outside their
apartment, hadn't she? She could do this. She needed a little
more faith in herself. A little more starch in her backbone, as the
heroines claimed in the historical romance novels she loved
reading.

"Of course, I do have an offer to become a female singer in a
country band." Lydia burst into laughter at Emily's horrified
expression.

"You cannot be serious!"

"Just have to say yes." Lydia paused to take a sip of her latte.
Emily's face had paled. "Pack a bag and hit the road."

"Lydia, you wouldn't!"

She shook her head. "Of course not. I'm teasing you. But I was
offered the gig. There's one problem though… I'm sort of seeing
one of the chefs at work."

"A catering chef?"

"His name is Warren Chamberland and he's one of the sous
chefs. Very goal-oriented. Even more handsome than ambitious.
Which is saying something." Lydia laughed and related the story of
how she met him for the first time.

"Quite the story to tell your grandchildren some day."

"Em!" Lydia shook her head and then finished her drink. She
checked the time on her cell phone. "I need to get to the grounds.
I'm working a shift at the Bannock Booth in an hour."

"I'm heading home to do laundry." Emily winked. "Want
to trade?"

"No, no, no. With all the clothes you own, you probably

haven't done laundry in a month!" Lydia hugged her friend. "I'll take serving the public over that any day."

"Wise choice," Emily admitted. "And good luck with the hunk. I want to meet him one of these days."

"I'm certain you will."

Emily wagged her finger at her. "And you *are* returning to school with me in the fall. We're going to continue this conversation until you see reason."

"Got to run." Lydia waved as she hurried toward the exit. If all it took was talking about her problems and fears to make them disappear... Or the wave of a magic wand... Where was a fairy godmother when you needed one?

Even her beloved grandfather had been at a loss as to how to help her with this problem.

LATER THAT AFTERNOON after her shift at the Bannock Booth, Lydia strode down the midway, searching for a sign of her grandfather who'd agreed to meet her for a cold drink and a few words.

"Lydia!"

She whipped around and spotted him standing by a refreshment stand near the mini donut booth. He loved those greasy treats!

"Lemonade, okay?" Bernard Crowchild called.

"Perfect, thank you." She found vacant seating at one of the picnic tables near the booth and saved a spot across from her.

"Here you go." The elder set the cups down and then seated himself. "How is my girl today?"

Lydia sipped the cold drink and sighed. "Feeling completely overwhelmed with all these commitments, as usual." Her grandfather had helped raise her, especially after school when her parents were at work. The kindly old man was her favorite person in the world, and she could tell him anything.

"Working at the Indian Village?" Grandfather wore a light blue plaid shirt under the familiar beaded deerskin vest that Grandmother had made for him years ago.

Lydia nodded. "Just finished at the Bannock Booth. Now, I have to dash over to Auntie's vendor booth and help her sell her native crafts. She was so busy yesterday, Mom decided her sister needed help. Mom also mentioned painting displays?"

Her grandfather shook his head. "Don't ask me. I can't keep up with my daughters anymore."

"I worked late at catering last night and I'm so tired I can hardly see straight. Now, it'll be another late night." Lydia polished off her lemonade. "Do you want another one, Grandfather?"

"No, this is fine."

"I'm getting another." Lydia hurried over to the booth and bought another drink. She settled back in her spot and took a sip. "It's way too hot today."

"I agree, but it's better than pouring rain."

"Yes, you're right." Lydia smiled. Kind black eyes looked at her from beneath bushy gray eyebrows. Two long silver braids hung well past his shoulders and crinkled smile lines marked his face and spoke of his sense of humor. He'd taught her some of the Sarcee language and customs, and he'd told her stories which instilled in her a feeling of belonging and pride in her heritage. No other person had made such an impression on her; he'd helped to mold her into the person she was today.

"How are you getting along with your mother?"

"We've talked. I hope she keeps her word and doesn't volunteer me for anything else." Lydia sipped her drink. "I warned her I would be spending time with Emily. We have tickets to see the chuckwagon races one night and an afternoon rodeo. And we're not missing the Luke Bryan concert for anything."

"And you shouldn't. You work hard, my girl. You deserve time for fun." Grandfather took her hand. "Keep talking to your mother.

Remind her you're twenty-five years old. Explain what your plans are and that you're in charge of your life now."

"Easier said than done. She doesn't always listen to me no matter how many times we talk," Lydia complained. "And speaking of plans… I ran into Malcolm Jack. Do you remember him?"

Grandfather's face lit up. "I do remember him. Always respectful, called me Mr. Crowchild and your parents Mr. Simpson and Mrs. Simpson-Crowchild. Helped elders by providing car rides to doctor appointments and trips into the city."

"Yes, that was Malcolm." Lydia smiled. "He's taller, not so skinny, but he seems like the same person he always was. He offered me a job as singer in the country band he plays in. He's a drummer. Goes by Sticks now," she added laughing.

"You, a singer?"

"I know. The idea is absurd. And I'm not certain why Malcolm thinks they need another singer. I heard their lead singer performing at a wedding I served at. He was so good."

Grandfather shook his head. "And you are seriously considering this?"

"No way. Malcolm and I are friends." Lydia met her grandfather's eyes and she smiled. "Besides, I'm seeing one of the chefs at Stampede Catering. I don't know what Mom will think about that."

"Is this man white?"

Lydia nodded.

"Well, if you truly like this boy and your mother creates problems for you, remind her that she married a Caucasian man named Samuel Simpson against my wishes. But they were so in love. Eventually, it warmed my heart to see them so happy. And then he died so young." Grandfather shook his head. "The heart rules us. If you like this young man, then you continue seeing him. Maybe he's the man for you. Maybe not. But it should be your decision."

"Thank you, Grandfather." Lydia felt herself beaming. "I still have to tell Mom how I feel about the nursing though."

"You haven't told her what you shared with me? Your indecision? Your fears?"

Lydia shook her head. "No, Grandfather. I'm too chicken."

Bernard Crowchild burst out laughing. "Oh, my girl. You will tell her when the time is right."

"If Mom knew how undecided I am about my life, she would be extremely disappointed in me."

The elder patted her hand. "Decide on your priorities and set limits. You must learn to say 'no'. This is a lesson I myself took years to learn. But when you realize you won't be here forever, you decide what is most important to *you*, and then you let go of everything else."

"Like storytelling?" Lydia squeezed his hand. "I watch your face while you tell stories about the animals and warrior stories, and I know you love it."

Grandfather smiled. "Yes, telling the stories of our people is very rewarding for me. And I enjoy it very much."

Lydia straightened in her seat. "So, say 'no'. I will try doing this."

"Good for you. No more suffering from PEBM." The elder winked at his granddaughter.

"PEBM?" she echoed.

"Pleasing everybody but me." He finished his lemonade. "Starting today, my girl, you should change that."

Lydia laughed. "Elders are so wise. I believe you're right."

# CHAPTER 8

Monday
Day four of Stampede

*W*arren closed his eyes and took a deep breath. He'd been on the run since early morning. Stampede week meant fourteen-hour days, late nights, and little sleep. By the end of the ten days every year, he wanted to sleep for a week. This year was shaping up to be no different.

He hauled the tub of raw whole chickens out of the walk-in refrigerator and set it on the prep counter. He paused for a second, his best boning knife in hand, then dug the first bird out of the tub and started cutting it into pieces. He needed to get these prepped and cooked asap.

"Hey, Warren, what's up?"

Warren glanced over at Nick. "Just working on tonight's menu."

Nick gasped. "Oh, crap, man! What did you do?"

"What do you mean?" Warren frowned.

"Look at your hand!" Nick pointed and dashed toward him.

Warren dropped his gaze to his work station and gasped, dropping his boning knife which clattered onto the floor. Blood dripped from where he'd cut himself when Nick had distracted him, the pain not registering in Warren's mind yet. "Hand me a towel or something!" Warren shouted. Dammit anyway. How the hell had he managed to do this?

"What's all the noise in here?" their boss inquired, entering the kitchen. The executive sous chef took one look and his expression clouded. "What the hell?"

"I know. I screwed up." Warren grabbed the towel from Nick and wrapped it around his hand.

"You need to see medical," the boss suggested, hands on hips.

Warren noticed Nick had disappeared out the kitchen doors. Medical staff were stationed throughout the grounds during Stampede and perhaps he'd gone to find someone.

"How did this happen?"

"I… I was in a hurry. I didn't sharpen my knives. I guess Nick distracted me when he entered," Warren admitted, noticing the blood darkening already and pressing more firmly.

His superior threw up his hands. "You're kidding me, right?"

Warren glared at his boss, rethinking the response that had almost slipped past his lips. He considered it best to remain silent.

"Didn't sharpen your knives. And cutting raw chicken on top of it!"

"Yeah."

"By forgetting to sharpen your knife, were you hoping to bleed to death from the cut? Or do yourself in with infection in the wound from raw chicken rampant with bacteria?"

Warren couldn't meet his boss's eyes. He'd screwed up big time and he deserved everything the man accused him of. This wasn't going to win him any points for his next performance review.

His boss scoffed, "Chamberland, I expected better of you."

Warren shook his head. Classic beginner mistake. "I expected more of myself," he whispered.

Lydia raced into the room and headed straight for Warren. "Nick said you cut your hand?"

The executive sous chef pointed to the victim with blood leaking out of an extremely sodden towel.

Lydia inhaled sharply. "Warren, what did you do? Thank goodness, Nick has gone to find someone from medical."

"It probably needs a couple of stitches. It'll be fine," Warren ventured. But even he didn't believe the words coming out of his mouth.

"Here." A line cook handed Lydia two more hand towels.

Lydia wrapped the hand again, adding the towels atop the others, taking over from Warren and holding the towel in place herself and tightening her grasp. "We need to stop the bleeding," she instructed Warren. "Medical can determine if we need to drive you to a hospital."

"Hospital?" he blurted, grimacing. The hand hurt more with her gripping it than it had when he'd done it. And he couldn't go to any hospital, he had work to do.

"You're a professional chef. How did you manage to cut yourself so badly?" Lydia met Warren's eyes.

"I was in a hurry. I didn't sharpen the knife."

Lydia shook her head. "You should go to the hospital."

Warren's mouth dropped open. "But it's Stampede. I need to be here to—"

"To contaminate everything we're preparing for guests?" the executive sous chef interjected. "Not damn likely!"

"But I…" Warren quit while he was ahead after catching a glimpse of his boss's murderous expression.

"You should have been more careful." Lydia touched his cheek. "Someone get me another towel, please. I hope medical gets here soon."

Just then, a pair of paramedics hired for Stampede entered the room and took over. Lydia stepped aside.

"How did this happen?" the male inquired.

Lydia explained that Warren's knife had slipped and they'd

attempted to stop the bleeding. "I don't know if an artery was hit, but there's a lot of blood."

Warren leaned against the kitchen worktable, feeling a little woozy. He couldn't meet Lydia's eyes. He felt like a damn fool already, and he wouldn't admit in front of Lydia that he was feeling a little light-headed. Blood loss? Nerves? Or was salmonella rampaging through his system already?

"What's your name?" the male paramedic inquired.

"Warren Chamberland," he muttered.

The paramedic met his eyes. "Your vitals are good, and someone needs to drive you to the hospital for stitches." The paramedic gazed around the room.

"I'll drive him." Lydia volunteered, then added, "I need to text my boss for permission to leave."

"I'll clear it with him," Warren's boss chimed in.

Lydia paused.

Warren touched her arm, knowing she was worried about leaving without clearing it with her own boss. "It will be okay," he said.

"Are you parked at a C-train station, Lydia?" Nick asked.

"No, I'm in the parking lot a block or so over." She met Warren's eyes, "Can you walk that far?"

"Yeah, no problem," he replied, without any hesitation. He hoped he wasn't lying to her.

"Give me your keys and I'll drive it to the entryway to the grounds. It will be quite a bit shorter distance for Warren to walk."

"I'll get my keys and purse and I'll be right back." Lydia raced out of the room.

Within five minutes she returned. She had to have run the entire way. She handed Nick her keys. "It's parked over about two rows, not far from the entrance."

"I'll find it. See you outside in a couple minutes," Nick said, racing out of the room.

"Take him to Rockyview Hospital," the on-site medic

instructed Lydia, while covering Warren's hand in a large plastic bag to accommodate the towels wrapped around his hand.

Lydia nodded. "Okay."

"Keep the pressure on it."

Warren nodded, tightening his grasp outside the plastic covering. He still felt a little light-headed. Thankfully, he'd been working in the BMO kitchen and he hadn't far to walk to the ground's entrance.

He followed Lydia outside, her arm wrapped around his. He made it across the lot, wending his way between a variety of tents. Several people gaped at him, but no one stopped them to chat. Lydia held the passenger door open for him, and Warren tumbled into the seat. Nick reached across and fastened the seatbelt for him.

"Good luck," Nick offered.

"Thanks," Warren muttered.

"No, problem." He shut the door.

Lydia hurried around to the driver's side and settled into the driver's seat which Nick had vacated a moment ago. "You're not going to puke or anything, are you?" she inquired while fastening her own seatbelt.

Warren shook his head. "I don't have a problem with blood. Ever deliver a calf?"

Lydia laughed. "Point taken. Keep your hand wrapped around the bag. And please don't get blood all over my leather seats."

"Yes, Miss Simpson-Crowchild." Warren glanced over at her. "I wouldn't think of it."

She reached across the console and touched his hand. "You'll be fine."

"I know," he whispered.

Soon, they were on their way.

Twenty minutes later, they arrived at the Rockyview Hospital. Lydia parked at the ER doors, released her seatbelt, and hopped out. She hurried around to the passenger side. Warren took a deep breath; he could do this. He stepped out of the vehicle. But a bout of light-headedness engulfed him as they entered through the Emergency doors. He flopped against the wall to prevent himself from falling on his face. He closed his eyes in hopes the dizziness would pass. Man, he prayed nobody thought he was drunk!

Lydia gasped and grabbed his good arm. "Warren, are you okay?"

He nodded, and after a few seconds passed, he opened his eyes.

A nurse hurried over, maneuvering a wheelchair with her. "Here, use this, sir."

Warren shook his head, thankful for the support of the wall. "I'll be okay in another minute or two."

"Sit down!" Lydia insisted.

He frowned but collapsed onto the seat as he was told.

"It's the biggest, strongest men who faint most often in these situations." The nurse pointed to the wad of blood-soaked towels wrapped around his hand covered with the plastic bag.

"Exactly," Lydia scoffed. "Really."

"What's more embarrassing, sir? Sitting in this chair or having people staring at you when you're spread-eagled on the floor?"

"I wasn't going to try to catch you." Lydia smacked his shoulder.

Warren had to admit she had a point. But he felt his face redden as he was wheeled inside, hoping no one he knew saw him in this contraption. If they did, he had no one to blame but himself. Then he grimaced, realizing he required a good attitude adjustment. Some guys spent a lifetime in a wheelchair, and no one thought less of them for it. He sat a little straighter, needing to get it together.

Thankfully, the ER wasn't too busy today. A nurse took his vitals and then wheeled him over to the desk for processing. Lydia helped him extract his health care card from his wallet. Soon, he'd been processed.

"I'm going to put my SUV in public parking. I'll be right back." She leaned over and pecked his lips.

"See you in a few minutes." He watched her dash away, feeling deserted. How had she become so vital to his life in such a short time?

The same nurse wheeled Warren into an ER room. He was settled on a hospital bed in a curtained-off enclosure. A couple minutes later, a nurse had taken his blood pressure and pulse again before disappearing. Now, he was lying here applying pressure to his throbbing hand, waiting to see a doctor. Even lying down, he still felt a little woozy. Settled against the pillows at his back, he stared at the ceiling.

Why hadn't he taken a few minutes and sharpened that damn knife? He knew better. How often had he heard his father warn him *shortcuts never save time.* And the culinary instructors had issued identical warnings against using unsharpened knives. Rancher, chef, cop, firefighter, anyone. Same rules applied. No shortcuts! And he sure as hell couldn't blame his co-worker for this. Nick hadn't surprised him when he entered the kitchen. Warren shook his head. The knife had slipped; this was all on him.

Hopefully, his boss wouldn't reconsider his carelessness and fire him. What a black mark on his resume if that happened!

The cloth partition parted and a young male doctor wearing a white lab coat entered, holding a patient chart. A different nurse accompanied him and stood by Warren's bedside. Lydia slipped into the room and rushed over to the other side of his bed. She smiled at him and slipped her arm around his shoulder, squeezing gently. A silent show of support.

"I'm Dr. Pillay. What is your name, sir?" He looked up from the chart.

"Warren Chamberland. Middle name Idiot," he answered, still applying pressure to his hand.

The doctor met his eyes, the corners of his mouth turning up slightly. "Doesn't say that on my chart."

"Warren David Chamberland," Warren replied. The doctor's accent had him stumped. Maybe South African.

"Date of birth?"

"September 14, 1987." Warren shifted into an upright position on the narrow hospital bed, grimacing when he moved his injured hand. Lydia reached out to help him.

"Are you okay?" she whispered.

He nodded.

The doctor set the chart on the end of the bed and donned a pair of gloves. He reached for Warren's arm, removed the plastic bag and then carefully unwrapped the blood-soaked towels. The whole mess was tossed into a nearby garbage can.

"Can you set up to irrigate the wound, please? And I'll require more gauze." The doctor nodded toward the young nurse standing on the opposite side of the bed. She didn't appear much older than the doctor. What happened to all the gray-haired physicians and middle-aged nurses Warren recalled his mother taking him to when he was a kid? He bet none of these people handed out lollipops or superhero stickers to well-behaved patients anymore.

"Certainly." The ER nurse busied herself with the preparations.

The doctor glanced up for a moment. "You really did a number here, Warren."

"I'm a chef. I cut myself with a dull boning knife."

Warren glanced at Lydia, knowing she possibly thought him foolish. He'd scolded her for her carelessness, the night they collided in the BMO hall. To her credit, she hadn't said a word in the kitchen. He'd probably fallen in love with her then and there.

The doctor examined Warren's palm. "The bleeding has stopped. I don't think there'll be damage to the bone. Although the cut is deep, it appears to run the same direction as the tendons. So I don't believe you've severed a tendon."

"That sounds promising," Lydia whispered, wrapping her hands around his arm.

"Um… I was cutting raw chicken at the time," Warren admitted, meeting the doctor's eyes.

"I read that on your chart." An unspoken tsk tsk was evident in the doctor's expression. "In any case, we'll start you on antibiotics right away."

Warren nodded. The doctor must know what he was doing. Perhaps the situation wasn't as bad as he'd feared.

"Let's have you go through a series of hand movements to check for tendon damage. Then we'll decide from there."

For several minutes, Warren endured the hand movement testing, grimacing more often than he'd like to admit. Lydia hadn't left his side. But the wound had started bleeding again!

"My hand's bleeding," Warren complained. "This is making things worse not better."

"Not at all," the doctor argued. "Bleeding is good because your biggest risk is infection. Is your tetanus shot up to date?"

"Probably. Cut myself with an axe last fall. Got one then," Warren explained, grimacing again as the doctor probed the wound.

"We'll check your records to be sure. Now, I'll clean the wound and then have a supervisor examine it."

"A supervisor?" Warren blurted.

"I'm only a resident. I'm not certain if I should suture your hand or not, given the risk of infection."

Warren sat, stunned. Had he heard correctly. "What do you mean *if I should suture your hand*? That's why I came here. I need stitches. I have to get back to work ASAP."

Lydia gave him a look that shouted, *listen to the doctor!*

The doctor straightened his back. "Mr. Chamberland, I don't think you realize how serious this could have been. And you certainly aren't out of the woods yet."

"What happens if I don't get stitches?" Warren swallowed hard. He needed an answer, but he felt certain he wasn't going to like it. Why hadn't he taken a few minutes and sharpened that damn knife! He met the doctor's eyes, clasping Lydia's hand. Thankful she'd come with him.

"We have two choices here. If my superior is worried about

infection, we'll irrigate the wound and then cover it with medicated gauze and not stitch it, providing it doesn't continue to bleed. The gauze must be changed regularly and the wound be monitored for infection. Depending on how deep the wound is and how often it breaks open, the healing could take weeks."

Warren felt his face pale. *Weeks?* No way would he be able to work with an open wound covered in gauze! What was this doctor thinking?

"What's the other option?" Warren ventured.

"If the supervisor deems it plausible, we'll stitch the wound. It should heal more quickly, but we would still monitor for signs of redness or swelling. And if the antibiotics don't prevent or cure any infection, there is always the possibility down the road you'll require a drain. And we can't rule out the need for physio later on, but we'll consider that option as we go."

Warren slumped against the pillows. *Open wounds? Weeks to recover? Physio?*

Could this day get any worse?

Lydia took his face in her hands. "Look at me."

He gazed into her eyes.

"Take a breath. It will be okay." She leaned over the bed and wrapped her arms around him. "You'll survive this. Truly you will."

How had he gotten so lucky, finding a wonderful woman like Lydia?

# CHAPTER 9

*A*fter what seemed like hours, Warren learned that the knife had missed damaging vital tendons and nerves. And the resident's supervisor had determined, despite the risk of infection, they wouldn't go the route of a drain. Warren suspected he'd be popping antibiotics like candy, but that he could do. Willingly. More than willingly. Religiously. He wouldn't risk losing his career. Or even death, as he'd been warned. These medical people didn't pull any punches!

"Okay, we'll thoroughly cleanse the wound and then I'll stitch you up." The doctor met his eyes. "This is serious, but it could have been much worse. You were lucky today. Keep those knives sharp!"

"Yes, sir. I've learned my lesson." Warren sighed. He'd tested the blade by scraping the edge with his thumb like some darn housewife, and the knife had felt sharp enough. He wouldn't be making that mistake again. "I sure as hell didn't save any time today by skipping the sharpening."

Lydia held his hand while the resident stitched up the other one, using dissolving sutures inside and stitches requiring removal in a week or so on the outside. Although they'd used a local anesthetic and he couldn't feel a thing, Warren preferred looking into

Lydia's eyes than watching the doctor at work. Pain free finally, he'd dozed off for a half hour, but Lydia hadn't left his side. He couldn't believe she'd stayed here with him the entire time.

Throughout this ordeal, it seemed a dozen people had warned him about the signs to watch for. Increased pain, fluid draining or pus, redness or swelling, fever and a feeling of malaise. Was he forgetting something? Man, he hoped not. Catching a problem early was too important. Hell, he'd probably be checking for signs in his sleep!

"How long will I be off work?" Warren asked the question foremost in his mind, not certain he would like the answer.

"I'd suggest you stay off work for a week. When you see your doctor to have the stitches taken out, he or she can decide. But unless you can wear gloves all the time in the kitchen—and I do mean ALL the time—you can't work until then." The doctor met his eyes. "The cut went deep. Seriously, make an appointment for re-evaluation in a week, either here or with a family doctor. They might consider physio at that time."

Warren nodded. How the hell would he fit in physio with his hectic schedule? But losing even a small percentage of the use of his hands was unthinkable. His hands were his career. His life. "I'll do whatever you think is necessary."

"Good answer," Lydia added.

"She's smart. You'd be wise to listen to her." The doctor smiled at her, pulling off his gloves. Job complete. Then he glanced at Warren. "Now, I'll ensure your paperwork is complete and you'll be free to go."

"Thanks, Dr. Pillay." Warren shook goodbye with his good hand. Thank goodness, he'd been given the okay to go home. He couldn't wait to get out of here.

Lydia leaned over and kissed him. "I'll fetch my SUV while the doctor ensures your paperwork has been done. I'll meet you out front."

Warren nodded. "Okay. And thanks for staying."

"Of course." She slipped out of the room.

Ten minutes later, Warren headed for the main entrance to meet Lydia. He waited in comfort, his hand still numb from the local. And the dizziness had passed. He stuffed the prescriptions for Tylenol 3 and for two different antibiotics into his pants pocket, planning to fill them at the drugstore near his apartment block.

A whole bloody week off work! Damn, damn, damn. He couldn't miss the duration of Stampede, the busiest time of the year. Would his hand possibly recover sooner?

Warren spotted Lydia pulling up in her SUV and he hurried outside so she wouldn't get a ticket for stopping there. He yanked open the passenger side door and crawled inside. "Thanks for doing this. I mean it. I really appreciate it." He reached back and grabbed the seatbelt with his good hand, and after some maneuvering, he finally snapped it into place.

Lydia pulled away from the hospital toward the set of lights on 14th Street and then headed north. "You want to hit a drive-through? Get something to eat before you go home?" There were several places to eat in or get takeout from on the other side of 16th Avenue.

"Yeah. A burger or something. My treat. And I need to fill a couple of prescriptions."

"So, the anesthetic's still working?" Lydia inquired, glancing his way and then returning her attention to the road.

Warren nodded.

"Okay. No problem. Food and meds. We've got this."

Lydia turned down 16th and then she heard Warren chuckling. "What's so funny?"

"You were singing along with Dolly Parton."

Lydia felt her face redden.

"I have to agree with that drummer. What's his name? Malcolm? You're a great singer."

"All my singing will be done in this vehicle," Lydia clarified.

"So you're not going pro?" Warren met her eyes for a moment.

She returned her gaze to the road. "Not happening."

"Glad to hear it," he muttered.

Fifty minutes later, prescriptions filled and takeout bag in hand, Warren stepped inside his apartment with Lydia on his heels.

"Nice apartment." Lydia peeked into the kitchen and then followed him into the living room.

"Thank you. One bedroom. Affordable. Close to work."

"About the same size as the two-bedroom place Emily and I share." Lydia settled onto the sofa.

"These painkillers are working. Don't feel any pain. Why couldn't I have returned to work?" Warren lamented, slumping into his recliner.

"Right. And pop out every suture the doctor put in your hand?" Lydia shook her head.

"The kitchen might be short-handed."

Lydia leaned back. "Forget it. The almighty Chef Chamberland is not indispensable. Stampede Catering will survive quite well without you."

Warren set his takeout meal on his lap, and with some difficulty worked the paper bag open with his good hand. He frowned at the inconvenience, using the fingertips on his bandaged hand to assist in unwrapping the burger.

He took a big bite; he was starving. He set the burger on the napkin and reached for a handful of fries, reluctant to use the damaged hand. "Could you grab me a beer out of the fridge, please?"

"Actually, no. I read your prescriptions. You're on high-test painkillers and two powerful antibiotics as well," Lydia reminded him. "I'm a student nurse, remember. Adding in booze is a sure-fire recipe for side effects."

Warren slumped against the back of his chair. All right, maybe she had a point.

Lydia leapt off the sofa, searched through his kitchen cupboards and returned a minute later with a cold glass of water. "This or nothing."

"Thanks." He accepted the drink she offered and took a couple gulps before setting the glass down and returning to his burger. He couldn't afford to jeopardize the effectiveness of the antibiotics, and getting a double buzz on booze and painkillers certainly wasn't a good idea. He'd better take it easy, and remain beer free, for now.

"Don't you have to be somewhere, Nurse Lydia?"

She laughed out loud. "You're such a prize. Why are men rotten patients when they're sick? My pleasure driving you to the hospital and seeing you home safely."

"Yeah, thanks." Warren grabbed the remote and met her eyes. If he felt better, he'd offer to show her his bedroom. But he doubted she'd be in favor of a tour anyway. Or anything else. They hadn't known each other that long. She didn't seem the type of girl who'd jump into the sack with a guy she only dated a couple times. "Sorry about my mood. I'll watch an afternoon ball game or something. I'll take my medicines. No beer. I'll be a model patient."

"Good to hear. And an improvement over this feeling-sorry-for-myself thing you have going on."

He shrugged. "Yeah, you're right. But I hate missing work."

Lydia stood and crossed the floor, leaning down and kissing him on the lips. "Take care, Warren, and I'll see you at work when your hand has recovered."

She started to head for the door, but Warren tossed the takeout bag aside and reached for her with his good hand. He pulled her onto his lap and kissed her thoroughly. Finally, they came up for air, both of them breathing heavily. "Your kisses could cure me of the plague," he whispered.

She scrambled off his lap. "Oh no. Enough kissing. You need your rest."

"A nurse should never desert her patient." Warren winked at her as she hurried across the room.

"Nice try." Lydia dug her cell phone out of her purse. "What's your cell number so I can check up on you?"

He chuckled. Man, he loved her. Could that be possible? So soon? He recited the digits while she keyed them into her cell phone.

Warren waved. "Bye. I'll talk to you soon."

"You be good," she called, closing the door behind her.

Like his father, Warren had never been one to sit around doing nothing. More than likely, Lydia would be seeing him at work sooner than she expected.

# CHAPTER 10

Tuesday
Day five of Stampede

Following the smudging ceremony, Bernard Crowchild related the story about skunk and the white stripe on his back, the Tsuut'ina elder surrounded by a group of spellbound listeners. As captivated as the others, Lydia smiled, having heard the story, one of her favorites, dozens of times. She'd grown up at her grandfather's knee, listening to his storytelling. The scent of sweetgrass still hung in the air, and Lydia inhaled deeply and closed her eyes, savoring the reminder of her youth. So familiar. So comforting.

Lydia recognized the importance of telling and retelling these stories. First Nations youth learned about their history from stories told by the elders. People from other cultures learned the First Nations ways and ancient beliefs, and hopefully, they gained a greater understanding and new tolerance of her people from listening to these stories. She believed developing an understanding and acceptance for any cultural differences was always promising.

"Hello, Lydia," a deep male voice whispered next to her ear.

She whipped around and recognized another boy she'd known in high school. He stood over six feet tall, had grown a trim mustache, his chest was thicker and he appeared a little heavier than he was back then, but she'd know him anywhere.

"Raymond! What are you doing here?" she whispered, motioning her old friend to follow her.

Lydia stepped away from the storytelling area and Raymond followed her. He wore knee-length khaki shorts, a tan collared golf shirt and sandals. He couldn't be working on the grounds. Must only be attending Stampede.

"I ran into your mother over at the Bannock Booth and she told me you would be here," he explained, smiling. "How have you been?"

"Good, thanks. I've completed my third year of nurse's training, well on my way to becoming an RN. And I'm volunteering for Stampede."

"Still competing at powwows? You were one heck of a good dancer."

"Usually every summer during July and August. I still love the competitions as much as ever," she replied, unable to admit her misgivings about continuing her schooling. But she smiled as an image of herself as a gray-haired elder still dancing to the drumbeat popped into her mind.

"How are you?" Lydia was interested; she hadn't see him in years, since he'd moved to Fort McMurray.

"Great. Still working in the oil patch."

A pretty blonde with twin boys who appeared to be about four years old wandered toward them. "Ready to go, honey?" she called.

"Yes, I am." Raymond slipped his arm around the woman. "Lydia, this is my wife, Rosemary."

"Pleased to meet you." Lydia smiled, shaking his wife's hand.

"You, too."

"And our sons, Ricky and Robbie. We kind of got stuck on 'R' names." Raymond laughed heartily, resting a hand on each boy's shoulder.

"Hi, guys." Lydia smiled at them, two peas in a pod. Except for their blue eyes, the identical children were the spitting image of their father.

Raymond appeared delighted with his family, smiling at his wife and tousling his sons' hair.

"Are you guys enjoying Stampede?" Lydia met eyes with the twins.

"It's awesome!"

"Yeah, I love the rides!" added the other one.

"Well, guys, we'd better get going." Raymond touched her arm. "Good to see you again, Lydia."

"You, too." She smiled and then met eyes with his wife and sons. "And it was nice to meet you guys, too."

"Sorry we have to rush off," Rosemary apologized. "We're meeting my brother and his wife at the dog show."

"Oh, the dog show! You're going to love it," Lydia predicted. "Those dogs are wonderful. And you don't want to be late."

"Let's go, Dad," the twins shouted in unison.

"We're right behind you." Raymond reached for his wife's hand and met Lydia's eyes. "Maybe we'll run into you again before Stampede ends."

"Drop by Indian Village anytime. If I'm not working, we'll hit the midway for a snack or something," Lydia suggested.

Raymond nodded. "Sounds like a plan."

They parted ways shortly before the storytelling was completed. Having finished her volunteer duties here, Lydia checked the time and her schedule on her cell phone. Next up, helping her auntie at her vendor booth from three o'clock until eight. Lydia wandered through Indian Village which was busy today, always a good sign.

She helped her aunt, both of them were run off their feet the entire time. "Am I finished now?" she enquired, as her aunt started packing her wares.

"Yes, Lydia. I couldn't have made it through the day without you. So many people were here today, and my sales were very good. Perhaps that is because of the pretty young lady helping me."

Lydia laughed. "Or the excellent quality of the beadwork that you do."

"Thank you, my girl. Now, you run off and do whatever you have planned for tonight."

"Okay. Let me know if you need help again."

"Your cousin, Shirley, will be here again tomorrow and for the rest of Stampede." Her aunt hugged her and kissed her cheek. "I'll be fine. Go. Have fun."

"Okay. Goodnight, Auntie."

As she strolled toward the Indian Village exit, Warren invaded her thoughts. She'd gotten his cell number; she needed to check on him. She dug her phone out of her purse and texted him.

*How are you doing?*

She held her breath, hoping he'd answer.

*Okay. Yeah, I'm doing all right. I think so.*

Lydia read between his words. All that was missing was an emoji sad face. Was he in excruciating pain? Or was he feeling alone? A little worried? Or maybe a lot?

*What's wrong? Need help? Can I bring food?*

She waited for his reply.

*Nick brought burgers. Went to work. Just bored.*

*Are you in pain?*

*No. Tylenol 3 working good.*

Decision made.

*I know what you need. I'm coming over.*

Lydia read her text again. That could be interpreted in a variety of ways.

*Get clothes on. See you soon.*

She headed for the Stampede train station to go and get her SUV.

~

WARREN FROWNED. "WE'RE GOING WHERE?" After sitting around talking, cuddling in his arms, and sharing kisses on his living room sofa for over an hour, she'd received a text message, and then announced they were going for a ride.

"You told me you were going stir crazy. We're going to the Grey Eagle Casino off 37th. My mother needs a ride home from Bingo." Lydia slipped into the driver's seat and clicked her seatbelt into place.

Warren grabbed the passenger side seatbelt. "I'm not used to a female driving me everywhere."

"Just until you're off those pain meds."

"Okay. I'm holding you to that." He leaned back in his seat.

"Besides, I love driving." She smiled over at him. "Been driving on the reserve since I was thirteen. Nearly killed me having to wait until I turned sixteen to get my license. And I got it, age sixteen and two days. Dad was so proud of my accomplishment. I'm glad he got to see me that day. He was killed on the job, two weeks later."

"I'm sorry you lost your dad so young." Warren glanced over at her. "It must have been a difficult time, right in the middle of high school."

"Yeah, it was. But I survived. Mom was great, even though she was grieving, too." Lydia navigated the SUV around a traffic circle and then pulled into the enormous parking lot outside the casino.

"It's busy. They might have some big-name entertainer performing tonight," Lydia speculated.

"I've never been here. Not a gambler." Warren followed her inside. "I don't even buy lottery tickets."

Lydia laughed. "A casino virgin. Maybe we should do something about that."

"I am *not* parting with my hard-earned money," Warren warned her.

Lydia disappeared to the other side of the casino lobby. He stared at a water feature wall: three smooth slate panels in gray, gold and teal tones—a beautiful eagle in flight was carved into the center one—that were lit and appeared to shimmer. He'd seldom seen anything like it. If he ever owned his own restaurant, he'd put one in it. What a conversation starter!

Soon Lydia returned. "Bingo isn't done yet. We should check out the casino for a few minutes while we wait."

"Really? Do you know the odds of winning in a casino?"

Lydia thought for a moment and then burst out laughing. "I haven't the foggiest idea. But I do know it's a heck of a lot of fun trying. Come on," she encouraged him, grabbing his good hand and tugging him toward the entry.

Warren paused outside the door, admiring the wildlife painting that was being raffled through Ducks Unlimited. His father helped out the conservation organization by dedicating a portion of the permanent wetland on the family ranch to the breeding of wild ducks and geese and whatever other wildlife made the area their home.

Warren followed Lydia inside, gazing at everything and feeling like a damn kid in a candy store. But if she'd intended to fix his boredom, it was working. They wandered around several machines that circled the perimeter, where people including many seniors played them. He noticed the cashiers were located at the back as they passed by a restaurant. There were tables spaced down the middle, probably for poker. Or maybe blackjack. He'd seen that in movies.

"So what do you want to try?" Lydia met his eyes, hugging his arm.

He shrugged his shoulders. "I have no idea."

"Choose a machine. And decide what you want to spend."

"They all look the same," he muttered, gazing toward the entrance. "Are you sure your mother isn't waiting for us?"

Lydia swatted his arm. "She's not waiting for us. Now pick one with an unusual name. I'll help." She wandered around the corner and he followed.

Warren read the fronts of the machines. "All of them have an unusual name."

"Here. What about this one… it's called Captain's Gold. Or this one is Cleopatra." She halted in front of one machine and then burst out laughing. "Okay, Warren. You *have* to choose this one."

He stepped closer and smiled. "Are you serious?"

"Dashing Dolphins," she read the name aloud. "You have got to admit it's unusual."

Warren threw up his hands. "Okay. We play with the dolphins. But just so you know, I can't swim."

Lydia burst out laughing. "That's swimming with the dolphins. Totally different thing."

Warren dug a twenty-dollar bill of his wallet. "Okay. What do I do?"

"Here, let me get you started."

With Lydia's help, he soon caught on how to play. What the expected outcome was he wasn't sure. He figured the true outcome would be a lot less money in his wallet. He played until Lydia screamed in his ear.

He froze.

What the hell had he done?

Had he broken the casino's damn machine?

He leaned back and met her eyes.

"You won!" she screamed.

Warren sat on the chair, speechless. Had he heard her correctly? He'd won? Really? He felt a grin sneaking across his face. Yes! Take that you dolphins!

"I won?" The words came out sounding as incredulous as he felt.

"Yes!" She swatted his arm. "Talk about beginner's luck."

A few minutes later, he stared at the cash fanned out in his hand. Four hundred and ten dollars. Holy hell! He never would have guessed the evening would take this turn of events.

"Mom!" Lydia called, waving.

A tall, slim woman with black hair and Lydia's smile strode toward them with purpose and confidence. She wore dark jeans, a short-sleeved white sweater, and a multi-colored silk scarf wound around her neck. This was her mother? Older sister maybe.

"Here you are, my girl. I wondered if you'd come in here to kill time while waiting for me."

Lydia hugged her mother. "Were you lucky tonight?"

"I won fifty dollars." Her mother laughed heartily. "Probably spent that much also, but it's the fun and the socializing that counts."

"Mom, I'd like you to meet Warren Chamberland. He's one of the chefs at Stampede Catering." Lydia beamed at him. "Warren, this is my mother, Melanie Simpson-Crowchild."

Warren stuck out his hand. "I'm happy to finally meet you."

"It's a pleasure to meet you, too." Her mother shook his hand, firmly and strongly but without causing pain like some women on a power trip had done to him in the past. This woman exuded power through confidence not from exerting her physical strength.

"Mom, Warren won big," Lydia whispered.

Her mother's eyes widened. "How big? If we go for coffee, is he buying?"

Warren laughed. "Oh yeah, I can spring for three cups of coffee. Even that fancy latte stuff your daughter loves."

Lydia squealed and hugged his arm. "Warren has never been in a casino before. And get this… he won four hundred and ten dollars."

"Congratulations!" her mother exclaimed, extending her arm and shaking hands with him again. "Make mine a double-double, please."

Lydia laughed. "Mocha latte for me."

"I remember. Let's go." Warren placed his hand on Lydia's back, guiding her toward the exit. Her mother walked on Lydia's other side.

For some reason, he hadn't expected Lydia's mother to be so accepting of him. Of course, Lydia had told him her father was Caucasian. Being accepted by her mother pleased him greatly. Who knew what the future would bring.

For now, he knew exactly how he intended to spend some of his winnings, besides buying tonight's coffees. First, he needed to survive this darn injury, and finish with Stampede.

CHAPTER 11

Wednesday
Day Six of Stampede

Lydia wrapped the Stampede-supplied apron around her waist and tied it securely in preparation for her shift. Marek Oil was holding a company event and Lydia had worked one of their luncheons before. The CFO, Marty Tate, stood with his daughter by the entrance to the room, finalizing plans with the catering supervisor.

Lydia wandered down the hallway, entered the kitchen, and strode across the floor to the hot food prep area. "What on earth are you doing here?"

Warren glanced at the Stampede ID tag clipped to his chef's coat. "Says I work here."

"You know what I mean. Your accident happened two days ago."

"And I'm all stitched up. Taking my antibiotics and doing fine. I even went out gambling last night." Warren stirred a large pot of something on one of the gas ranges.

"Didn't the doctor tell you to stay home?"

Warren nodded. "Said to take time off until I felt well enough to return. I felt well enough today."

"He meant take an entire week off *or longer* until you feel well enough."

"Not how I interpreted it," Warren muttered. "Stampede is the busiest time of year around here. Besides, if I need to lift heavy items like this soup pot, I'll get Nick's help with it."

"Have you replaced those bandages today?" Lydia couldn't believe he'd returned to work so soon.

"Yes and there's no sign of redness or other problems." He continued working but hadn't met her eyes.

"So you're not putting co-workers or customers in harm's way."

"I would *never* do anything to jeopardize anyone's health." Warren met her eyes. "I'm keeping it clean. Taking my meds. Doing what I'm suppose to do."

She shook her head. "Everything, except for taking time off work."

"I consider it doing my part during the busiest time of the year. Being responsible and carrying out my obligations to my employer."

"If you're determined to return this soon, then make certain your hand is okay." Lydia heaved a sigh. "Or I can drop by here and look at it for you."

"I can do it." Warren winked at her. "Unless you're using that as an excuse to see my handsome face every day."

Lydia wouldn't admit that the thought had crossed her mind. Her heart skipped a beat every time she laid eyes on him. And then it danced a tango with her ribcage when he kissed her, also causing her knees to weaken and her mouth to go dry. He seldom left her thoughts. She had to be falling in love with him.

"Why are you being all 'nurse-like' today? Have you made a decision about your training?" Warren glanced at her, waiting for an answer.

She closed her eyes for a moment before meeting his eyes and replying. "Not really. Honestly, I panicked a little when I first saw all that blood."

"So, do you panic when it's someone you care about that's bleeding? Or people in general?" He grinned at her.

Lydia looked into Warren's eyes. "At least I didn't burst into tears when you cut yourself."

"Progress."

"Baby steps." She left the kitchen, smiling.

Two hours later, Lydia broke the news to the pastry chef who was heading up her staff of three at this private event. "We're missing twelve."

"You don't have enough?" The young woman stood, appearing shocked.

"No. We're short twelve desserts," Lydia repeated.

The woman gaped. "We counted and we prepared four extra."

"Perhaps some guests already took a second serving. There isn't enough here for the far two tables." Lydia doubted the staff had miscounted, but the desserts had disappeared somehow.

The pastry chef nodded. "Hang on. It's vanilla ice cream and macaroons, some easy plating. I'll get another dozen made up right away." The woman dashed back toward the kitchen, calling to one of her assistants to follow her.

Lydia waited beside a support post. Dinner preparations in the kitchens always appeared to be utter chaos. How everyone knew what to do, what the other people were doing? How everything came together remained a mystery to her. How the kitchen staff managed to serve each course on time and in an orderly manner was beyond her comprehension. On occasion a blip occurred, like tonight. But that was easily remedied. Both the culinary and pastry chefs and their teams were so talented and professional, she couldn't be more impressed.

A few minutes later, the chef rolled a cart out and met Lydia's eyes. "Here. Get these out quickly. Everyone else is almost finished."

Lydia quickly distributed the desserts to the last two tables of guests waiting at the dessert station. Judging by their animated discussions centered around the latest chuckwagon racing results, they hadn't been miffed by the delay.

Bullet dodged.

Now, finish collecting the dirty dishes and returning them to the dishwashers, and she'd be out of here in another couple hours.

Lydia carried her tray topped with dirty dishes into the kitchen.

"That is *not* how it's done!" Warren shouted at one of the other servers.

Lydia had never seen the chef so flustered, verbally skewering anyone because of something they'd done wrong. Whenever they'd worked together before, he'd always remained cool under pressure, no matter what degree of culinary madness surrounded him.

Warren threw off his vinyl gloves and dragged his right hand through his hair. "Sorry, man," he muttered the apology.

The server's face had turned ghostly pale, and he glanced at Lydia who nodded toward the exit. The teenager dashed out of the kitchen.

"What was *that* all about?" she whispered, rubbing his back and staring into his eyes.

"Misplaced blame. I apologized." Warren spoke, eyebrows pinched.

"That little whatever-it-was that I witnessed wouldn't be due to your hand, by any chance?"

Warren's eyes widened. She'd nailed it.

"The pain is probably killing you right now. Maybe you should have listened to your doctor. Not returned to work so soon." Lydia tried her best to keep her voice non-judgemental. But as much as she loved him, he probably deserved the scolding.

A prominent vein in his forehead pulsed. She'd figured out the cause of his anger with the server, all right. And he hadn't liked it one bit.

"What's she talking about?" The executive sous chef inquired.

"Did you lie to me? You said your doctor told you the hand would be fine."

Warren met his boss's eyes, shoulders tensed. "I didn't lie. The hand will be fine. Good as new."

"Yeah, in time," Lydia blurted, before she could stop herself or consider the consequences.

"Chamberland, my office. Now!" His boss headed out of the kitchen, expecting Warren to follow him.

Warren shook his head and followed on his boss's heels, without a backward glance.

*For Pete's sake. When would she learn to shut her mouth? Keep her opinion to herself? What if she'd gotten him fired?*

Lydia returned to work, her stomach in knots.

*Please don't fire him. Please don't fire him. Please don't fire him.*

She repeated the mantra a thousand times in the next hour while clearing tables and completing innumerable trips to the dishwashing area. Still no sign of Warren.

Should she talk to his boss? She'd been present when the doctor suggested Warren not return to work for a week. But the doctor had also mentioned working with a glove on all the time. In her opinion, Warren had retuned to work early. But who better to know how his hand felt, but Warren himself.

*Damn, damn, damn. When are you going to learn to mind your own business, Lydia?*

With only three years of university and limited practical nursing training under her belt, Lydia's professional opinion didn't count for beans. Her eyes filled with tears. And she may have gotten someone she loved fired.

~

"CLOSE THE DOOR."

Warren complied with his boss's request. His mentor slumped onto his executive office chair and then waved Warren toward the armless vinyl chair on the other side of his ample desk. "Start explaining. And I'd better like what you have to say."

Warren doubted that would happen, especially if he told him the truth. Warren had interpreted the doctor's orders to his own advantage. He knew it, Lydia knew it, and his boss would realize it also.

Warren took a deep breath. "My hand is a little sore, but I've been taking Tylenol for that."

"What *exactly* did your doctor tell you?"

Warren glanced up at the ceiling. "He told me my hand would be fine. He prescribed antibiotics and painkillers." He didn't add that physio might be required, preferring to downplay the situation as much as possible.

"Chamberland, what aren't you telling me?"

Warren dragged his good hand down his face. Should he fess up that he'd probably returned to work much earlier than his doctor intended? Or he could skate around the issue. But what if his boss questioned his doctor about it? He'd have more explaining to do.

"The doctor said and I quote… *stay off work for a week.*"

His boss's mouth dropped open.

"He also said I couldn't work unless I wore a glove ALL the time," Warren muttered, holding up his gloved hand. "I can wear a glove."

His boss stared at him.

"Okay, I may have interpreted the doctor's instructions differently than intended." Warren slid forward in his chair. "But we're too busy during Stampede for anyone to be sitting at home watching sports on TV, playing nursemaid to a hand that is perfectly capable of working."

"Perfectly capable?"

"There's no sign of problems. I'm taking my antibiotics on time, every time. Couple of Tylenol and I'm good to go. And this glove hasn't left my hand since I got here." Warren twisted his wrist and waved his hand around, proving his claim. He didn't explain that he was probably on the strongest Tylenol they made.

His boss shook his head. "Well, you're here now. You might as well stay. Lord knows we can use you. But if you have any signs of a problem, get…your…butt…home!"

"Fair enough," Warren agreed readily, stifling the grin that threatened to appear on his face. Yes! He was staying!

"We reported the incident to Workers' Compensation. I'll hold off for a few days before I inform WCB that you've returned to work. Just in case…"

"Thank you." Warren leapt off the chair. No more damn worker compensation paperwork. Another bonus. "Two days downtime is enough for anyone." He headed out of the office before his boss had a change of heart.

Stepping through the doorway he heard his boss mumble something that sounded like *not for someone with a few brains in their head.*

Warren couldn't afford to take offense and raced to the elevator to return to the kitchen.

～

LYDIA SAT on the bench near the mini-donut booth, hoping Warren hadn't been fired today. She'd never crossed paths with him again and she hadn't heard anything discussed between her co-workers either. The Marek Oil luncheon had been a rousing success and the owners and executives were pleased.

But what had happened when Warren met with his superior?

She'd never forgive herself if he'd been fired.

"Can I join you?"

Lydia whipped around and met eyes with the person she'd been worrying about. "What happened with your boss?"

Warren clambered onto the picnic table bench and set his cold drink on the table. "He asked questions. He didn't like some of my answers, but he finally agreed I could stay. If I see any signs of trouble, I'm out of there until my hand is completely healed."

Lydia's breath escaped in a whoosh. She hadn't realized she'd been holding it. "Thank goodness. I was so afraid I'd gotten you fired."

Warren pulled a bottle of painkillers out of his backpack. He emptied two of them into his hand and downed them with a gulp of his drink.

"What's that?" Lydia pointed to his paper cup.

"Vodka, straight," he replied, grinning.

"Yeah, right." She laughed. "Okay I might have deserved that, but I'm concerned about you."

"Lemonade." Warren replaced the cap on the medicine and returned it to his backpack. "And I appreciate you worrying about me."

"Does it hurt much?"

"It's throbbing like hell and I can't wait for those pills to start working." Warren met her eyes. "I hate to do it during Stampede, but maybe I should ask for half shifts where possible."

"Your boss would understand. Probably be impressed that you recognize your limitations," Lydia speculated, sipping her drink.

Warren sighed heavily. "Yeah, but I hate to do it."

Lydia heard a strange noise, caught a glimpse of pink out of the corner of her eye, and turned to her right. A little girl about three or four stood a couple feet from their table, hugging a tattered brown teddy bear. Huge tears coursed down her chubby cheeks and her shoulders heaved with each sob.

Warren followed her gaze, clambered off his seat, and rushed over. "Sweetie, are you lost?"

Lydia followed on his heels.

The little girl nodded her head. "Yes," she whispered so softly Lydia almost couldn't hear.

Warren crouched down, lifted the little girl into his arms with his good hand, and then stood. "Don't cry. We'll help you find your mom, okay?"

One small arm wrapped around his neck in what resembled a vise grip.

"I need my daddy," she whispered. The little girl wore a pretty pink sundress with lacy white ruffles and matching pink sandals. Her long hair hung in loose curls held in place with pink butterfly barrettes. Someone loved pink.

"What's your name, sweetie?" Lydia patted the child's knee.

"Sherry. I'm three," she added, smiling through her tears.

Lydia suspected Sherry must have had a recent birthday.

Warren's gaze searched their surroundings. Lydia didn't hear anyone calling the child's name.

"What does your daddy look like?" Lydia muttered. Of course, the child didn't answer. He would look like daddy.

Lydia smiled as Warren held the child tighter, contemplating finding someone from Security. She noticed a large bandage on the little girl's arm. "Do you have an owie?"

Sherry had stopped crying, and she nodded her head.

"What happened?" Warren met the child's eyes.

"I got burn…ded," she whispered. "I was bad."

Warren looked into her eyes. "I don't think you were bad. I bet it was an accident."

Lydia blinked back tears, watching Warren comforting the little girl. So loving and tender, his concern genuine. She recalled him telling her he had nephews. He must be a wonderful uncle.

"Sherry!"

Lydia whipped around, hearing a man's voice calling the little girl's name. Easily six feet tall or more, with blond hair, wearing tan shorts and a white t-shirt, the man rushed toward them despite the flip flops on his feet.

"We found her. She's fine," Warren called.

"Thank goodness!" The man hurried over and the little girl extended her arms to him.

Warren handed the child over. Lydia nodded, obviously the man was her father. The man snatched the bear out of the air when it slipped out of Sherry's hand, and then he handed it to her.

Lydia met the man's eyes. "What happened?"

"I turned my back for a few moments while I was buying a lottery ticket." He shook his head. "I looked again and she was gone."

"And your heart stopped," Lydia added, smiling.

"You must have kids." He smiled at her.

"No. Lots of cousins and I've heard stories from my aunts." She stuck out her hand. "I'm Lydia."

"Two nephews," Warren added, shaking hands with the father. "I'm Warren."

"Richard," the father replied. "I can't thank you guys enough for finding her."

"Actually, she found us. We were sitting here and I heard her crying." Lydia touched Sherry's arm. "I'm a nursing student and I noticed we have an owie here."

"She toppled a cup of coffee onto herself." Richard grimaced. "I should have warned her that I'd set it on the table."

"Ouch," Warren exclaimed, holding up his hand. "I have an owie also."

The little girl's eyes widened and her mouth formed a small o. "Does it hurt?"

"Sometimes," Warren admitted. "But accidents happen."

Lydia smiled at the little girl. "See. You weren't bad. Only an accident."

"Of course not, honey. You're a very good girl." Richard hugged his daughter and then met Lydia's eyes. "Being a single parent is hard, but I'm trying my best."

Warren touched the man's arm. "I think you're doing okay. You have a darling little girl."

"Thank you. And thanks again for keeping her safe until I found her."

"You're welcome. We were seconds away from finding Security. Glad to help." Lydia waved as they headed down the midway.

"Goodbye," Warren called.

Sherry peeked over her father's shoulder and waved at them.

Warren and Lydia returned to their seats and sipped their drinks.

"Well, that was a bit of excitement," Warren muttered.

Lydia nodded and leaned her arms on the picnic table. "Good deed for the day done." A feel-good vibe engulfed her and she smiled.

"I guess I should get home before these painkillers put me to sleep." Warren yawned. "I'll catch the next C-train and hit the sack early tonight."

Lydia stood when he did. "I could drive you."

Warren shook his head. "No. We'd still have to take the train to get your vehicle. And then the drive to my place. It'll be quicker if I take the train. Besides, you must have plans."

"Yeah, I'm meeting Emily. We have tickets for the chuckwagons and grandstand." Lydia smiled. "I've been looking forward to it all day."

Warren leaned over and kissed her lips. "Then enjoy. I'm beat. I'm heading home."

Lydia kissed him again. "Take care of that hand."

Warren waved as he headed toward the train station.

Lydia watched him leave, admiring the way his jeans fit from the rear view. Her thoughts wandered to the episode with the little girl, and she reviewed how thoughtful and caring Warren had been with her. He'll make the perfect father some day.

"He might be stubborn, but he's a keeper," she muttered aloud, smiling. And then she headed toward the Harvest Building, the designated meeting place with Emily.

# CHAPTER 12

Early Thursday morning
Day seven of Stampede

After the chuckwagon races and Grandstand Show, Lydia had returned home with Emily to the Patrician Village apartment they shared during the school year, which was located on University Drive and an easy walk to campus. They'd cooked a frozen pizza, visited while they ate, and then made microwave popcorn and watched a movie. She couldn't remember the last time she'd had so much fun.

But Lydia had promised to spend the night at her mother's on the reserve to make plans in the morning for her grandfather's birthday next week. Lydia had forgotten all about it until her mother texted to inquire when she'd be arriving. Now, heading to her mother's place, Lydia turned onto southbound Crowchild Trail, the roadway named in honor of David Crowchild, a former Chief of the Tsuut'ina Nation. The clock on her dash indicated the time.

"Two a.m. already. Thank goodness, I don't have to work early tomorrow," she muttered. Her shift didn't start until noon.

The radio played, set to her favorite country station. She sang along with one of Reba McEntire's oldies. And then joined Shania Twain during the chorus of one of her releases, the only words she knew. Lydia cleared her throat, once, then again. Already her throat felt scratchy. Getting good? Obviously, Shania wasn't crooning about Lydia's singing career.

"You ladies have nothing to worry about. Lydia won't be the next big voice on the country charts any time soon." She laughed at herself. *Country singer? Even in a small band? Not in this lifetime.*

Continuing on toward her Glenmore Trail exit, she noticed a black Jeep up ahead wandering back and forth across the center line delineating Crowchild Trail's two southbound lanes.

"That a-hole must be drunk!"

Stunned by what she was witnessing and with her mind racing as she considered her options, she slowed as she drove past the old Currie Barracks on her right. She should call 9-1-1 and report that idiot!

Suddenly, the Jeep accelerated while attempting to pass a small red sedan up ahead. Abruptly, the driver of the Jeep steered back into the right lane, clipping the side of the sedan sending both vehicles spinning out of control.

"No, no, no!" Lydia slammed on her brakes.

A pickup truck flew past her and broadsided the sedan pushing it against the steel barrier separating southbound and northbound traffic. Both vehicles continued forward while the sedan scraped along the barrier for several feet, metal on metal sending sparks flying.

The Jeep careened onto the right shoulder and crashed into a light standard.

Lydia stopped and jammed the gearshift into PARK.

"Holy crap. What the hell? I've got to do something." Someone was certain to be hurt, especially the driver of that red car.

She grabbed her cell phone to call 9-1-1, hands shaking and heartbeat racing. She pushed the button on her cell phone but the screen remained black. Damn. She'd meant to charge it at the apartment but forgot. "No!" She tossed her phone onto the passenger seat.

She leapt out of her SUV and jogged toward the wreckage. A young man probably eighteen or nineteen opened the Jeep's driver side door and tumbled onto the ground. He stumbled to his feet, and then wandered into the middle of the road. A silver sports car slowed, swerved to miss him, and then sped up again.

"What the hell are you thinking? You idiot! Don't you realize there was an accident?" Lydia shouted at the departing set of tail lights. Any normal person would have stopped.

Ignoring the drunk driver from the Jeep, she glanced over at the pickup. The driver waved her toward the sedan.

"Call 9-1-1," she shouted and then raced over to the red car.

She poked her head in through the broken driver's side window, and gasped. Why hadn't the airbag deployed? The windshield had shattered and popped out, the adhesive giving way. An obviously pregnant woman was lying back against the driver's seat. Blood trickled down her face from a cut on her left temple. Her head had probably hit the driver's window when the pickup truck t-boned her vehicle's passenger side.

"Hello. Can you hear me?"

Nothing.

Lydia's training cut in. Deep breath. Airway – clear. Breathing – yes. Pulse – next. Don't move her head until assessed for spinal damage. She carefully checked the woman's carotid pulse. Thready but there. She sucked in another breath. Okay. She could do this.

"Can you hear me?" she asked again.

Silence.

The woman must be unconscious. Non-responsive but she was breathing on her own with a rapid heartrate. Okay.

She needed to check the woman's extremities to report as completely as possible to the first responders when they arrived.

"Someone, help me," Lydia screamed, struggling with the

driver's side door which had been crushed and twisted during the collision.

No one came.

*No, this can't be happening. I need to get inside!*

After three attempts, Lydia managed to yank open the driver's door. Thankfully, the pickup truck had broadsided the passenger side or the woman might have been killed instantly.

And then Lydia noticed a jagged glass shard sticking out of the young woman's left leg. Where the heck did that glass come from? Blood spurted everywhere. Had a main branch of the driver's femoral artery been sliced? Lydia felt faint, recalling the driver was pregnant.

And she would probably bleed out in a matter of minutes!

Killing both mother and unborn child.

"My wife called 9-1-1. Can I help you, miss?"

Lydia's head whipped up. An older gentleman poked his head in through the broken passenger side window. The woman would bleed to death before the ambulance arrived unless Lydia acted quickly.

"Take off your tie and give it to me," Lydia ordered.

He stood, appearing as shocked as if she'd asked him to strip naked.

"Tie. Now."

Without another second of hesitation, he fumbled with the knot and then he yanked his tie loose and pulled it off. "Here you go." He passed it over to her.

Lydia quickly secured the tie around the woman's leg above where the glass shard stuck out. "Thanks. I'm using it as a tourniquet to stem the blood flow." She should probably have apologized for yelling at him, but he'd disappeared. At least, someone had called 9-1-1.

She slipped out of her cotton hoodie to use it to stem the blood flow. *Don't remove the shard*, she told herself. She applied pressure to the wound near the shard, further staunching the bleeding.

"Where the hell is an ambulance?" she shouted.

She'd never been so scared in her life. Blood from the wound had stopped spurting out, but her hoodie had already become damp, and she was covered in blood.

"Somebody bring me a blanket, jacket, anything," she called over her shoulder, remembering to keep the patient in shock warm. They needed to get the woman to the Foothills Hospital Trauma Centre. And soon!

"Let me know the moment the paramedics get here!" she shouted again. Was anyone hearing her? Her head buzzed and her own heartrate hadn't slowed one iota. If she hadn't been young and healthy, she would fear the possibility of having a heart attack herself. Was she doing the right thing? Had she forgotten anything? A blanket? Hadn't she asked for a blanket? Her hands shook.

"Easy, girl. You're doing fine," the old fellow encouraged her.

"We need a blanket," she repeated the request.

Lydia stared at the woman, willing her to wake up. But then again, maybe it was best she remained unconscious. She wasn't thrashing about in pain or panicking at the sight of all the blood, making it more difficult for Lydia to apply constant pressure to the wound.

*How are you doing in there, little guy?* Lydia silently inquired of the unborn child, hoping the baby hadn't sustained an injury in the crash. Without a stethoscope to check for a fetal heartbeat, she felt totally helpless. She wished she had a third hand to feel the woman's abdomen to detect movement.

Finally, sirens could be heard in the distance, and Lydia sent a silent prayer of thanks heavenward. She noticed the woman's chest rising and falling; she was still breathing but taking shallow breaths.

Oh, no! What if she stopped breathing? How could Lydia perform CPR and apply pressure to the wound to keep the woman from bleeding to death at the same time? Her hoodie was close to completely soaked through.

"Where is the damn ambulance?" she shouted again.

"Here, miss, use this." The old gentleman handed her a cotton baby's blanket. "Belongs to one of my grandchildren. It's clean. I found it in the car."

"Thank you." Lydia quickly placed the tightly folded blanket on top of her sodden hoodie, never letting up on applying pressure despite her muscles screaming for relief. Moving the hoodie could rip open any clotting that might have occurred, freshly opening the wound. One mistake she wouldn't make.

The sirens drew closer. Tires screeched to a halt. At least two emergency vehicles had arrived. A fire truck always accompanied the ambulance, she recalled.

"Over here," the old gentleman called.

A second later, a paramedic in uniform stepped up to the driver's side and looked over her shoulder. "What happened?"

"Broadsided by the pickup truck," she blurted. "I think the Jeep's driver is drunk and wandering around here somewhere."

The paramedic raced around to the passenger side. The badly crumpled passenger door fell off when he yanked on it.

Lydia continued, "She's breathing, but shallow. No idea about her vitals. I put a tourniquet on her leg. I think a main branch of her femoral could be sliced. I've applied constant pressure." Lydia's voice caught. "I hope she's not bleeding out."

"You're doing great." The male paramedic climbed inside and opened his bag. "We'll stabilize her and then transport. Keep pressure on that wound."

"Okay," Lydia whispered, her hands shook slightly, muscles burning. For some reason, sirens started up again.

The first paramedic stabilized the woman's neck with a cervical collar. "Okay, it's safe to remove her from the vehicle," he called.

With their combined effort, the two paramedics removed the woman through the driver's side and laid her on a stretcher. A game of Twister required less acrobatics, but Lydia had managed to maintain constant pressure on the wound the entire time. Immediately, the paramedics established two IVs. They were treating two patients. One IV would be fluids and the second no doubt would be blood.

"Can we transport now?" the second paramedic asked.

"Yeah, I think so. This woman is coming with us and keeping pressure on the wound, freeing me to keep checking her vitals and checking for a fetal heartbeat while you drive," the first paramedic stated.

The other paramedic nodded and met eyes with Lydia.

"I can do that," she responded without hesitation.

"She probably saved this young mother's life." The paramedic was praising her.

Lydia's eyes welled, hearing his comment. Her muscles burned from applying pressure to the wound for all her worth. She wasn't quitting unless her damn arms fell off.

"Okay, let's go!" The paramedics hurriedly loaded the stretcher into the ambulance, Lydia applying pressure to their patient's wound and working in cooperation with them.

The doors slammed behind them and the ambulance raced through the night toward the Foothills Hospital.

Lydia closed her eyes and tilted her head heavenward. *Please, God, let us get her to the hospital in time to save her and the baby. And may that drunk driver rot in jail for the rest of his life!*

# CHAPTER 13

*A*t the Foothills Hospital, the ER doctors met them and took over. Lydia wiped her arm across her brow. She looked down at herself and bile rose to her throat. She looked like she'd been cast in a CSI murder scene on TV. So much blood!

"Are you okay?" A nurse approached her.

"I…I don't know. I… I think so," Lydia stammered.

Was any of this blood hers? No, she hadn't cut herself as far as she could recall. But that poor woman had lost so much blood. And how had the unborn baby fared? Lydia swallowed hard, feeling ill. Had she done enough?

What was Warren doing right now? Should she phone him? She needed strong arms around her. Yearned for a kiss to make everything all right again. She couldn't believe she'd thought of him, instead of calling her mother. Or her beloved grandfather. No, she'd wanted to be in Warren's arms, hear his comforting words whispered in her ear. She did love the handsome chef. More so than she'd been willing to admit to herself.

The nurse touched her arm. "Let's get you cleaned up."

Calling Warren would have to wait. Lydia accompanied the nurse down the hallway, her arms tingling as she regained feeling once again. The nurse flicked on a light switch as they entered a supply room.

"Here's a set of scrubs for you to wear. Change out of those blood-soaked clothes," the kindly woman said, dragging a pair of clean folded scrubs off a shelf.

"Thank you so much," Lydia whispered, her vision clouding with tears.

"You've had quite the night."

Lydia sighed. "You can say that again." She stripped off her jeans, t-shirt and undies. "Just burn these, please."

"Will do," the nurse said, handing her the clean clothes and then collecting the soiled garments from the floor.

Lydia donned the scrubs, at least two sizes too big. But that kept anyone from guessing she wasn't wearing a bra.

"Where are your shoes?"

Lydia stared at her bare feet, noticing them for the first time. "I… I was wearing a pair of flip flops. I guess I lost them somewhere between the accident scene and here."

The nurse handed her a pair of cloth booties worn over shoes in the OR. "Here, these are better than nothing."

Lydia slipped her feet into them, appreciating the warmth they provided. "Thank you again for your kindness."

The nurse patted her arm. "There's a sink here. Let's get your hands and face washed, too. And as for the kindness, you've earned it. You saved that woman's life."

"Thanks. Three years of nurse's training paid off," Lydia muttered. She quickly cleaned herself as best she could. What she wouldn't give for a nice hot shower. On second thought, every bone in her body ached and all she wanted was to fall into bed and sleep!

"Well, you'll make a wonderful nurse. Someone I would work a shift with any day." The woman smiled, leading the way out. Lydia felt herself blushing with the praise.

Five minutes later, Lydia slumped into a chair in the waiting room. She recalled someone had mumbled something about a ride.

She couldn't remember anything beyond the instructions to sit here for a few moments. Her eyes drooped but she forced them open again.

One of the paramedics had accompanied her to the seating area. "Are you okay?"

Lydia glanced up and met his eyes. "Um… yeah, I think so."

He smiled at her. "You do realize you saved that woman's life, probably her baby, too, right?"

She nodded, unable to speak or she might start crying. She'd never felt so tired.

"Here you go," the other paramedic offered her a cup of hot coffee.

Lydia accepted the Styrofoam cup. Without thinking, she took a sip, burning her tongue in the process. She squelched the curse word that threatened to escape her lips, wrapping the cup around her hands hoping the warmth would permeate her entire body.

"You were great. What's your name?"

"Lydia. Lydia Simpson-Crowchild."

The paramedic seated beside her sipped his coffee. "I'm Todd. Do you have some first aid or medical training?"

Lydia nodded. "Just completed my third year in the U of C's nursing faculty, to become an RN."

"It showed. You didn't panic and knew exactly what to do."

"Yeah, great work," added the second paramedic. "I'm Tim."

"Thank you." She sipped her coffee despite the sting to her tongue, not knowing what else to say.

Lydia closed her eyes, savoring the warmth of the hot drink which penetrated her weary bones and aching arm muscles while she considered what had happened tonight. She'd stepped up. She'd done what had to be done, putting into practice what she'd learned in her first three years of training. Simply leapt into action without a moment's hesitation. Without thinking about what needed to be done, just doing it. And doing exactly what was right.

She couldn't believe it!

She'd done it!

Lydia Simpson-Crowchild had saved two lives!

No emotional shutdown. And no tears!

Feelings of achievement and purpose blanketed her in a cocoon of comfort and contentment. Her future might have been determined tonight. Perhaps she was suited to the nursing field after all. She hadn't felt this happy or positive about her career choice in months!

"Excuse me, miss."

Lydia's eyes flew open. She hadn't realized she'd closed them.

"Are you Lydia?" An officer wearing a Calgary Police Service uniform stood in front of her, searching her eyes.

"Yes… That's me," she stammered. Now what? Having to complete reams of paperwork flashed through her mind.

He dragged a chair closer. "I understand you were the first person to come upon the accident."

"Actually, it all happened before my eyes." She straightened in the chair, dragging her aching body into a more upright position. She didn't feel respectful slumped in her seat, while discussing such a serious matter with the officer.

"We'll need you to provide a statement."

Lydia heaved a sigh. "Okay."

"You have the option of doing it now or in the morning."

"Now is fine." Lydia related everything she remembered while the officer took notes. "I noticed a driver swerving all over the road. I thought he might be drunk, so I slowed down. But I doubt the driver of that pickup truck could have anticipated what would happen and could have avoided hitting the sedan. I hope he isn't in trouble. But I don't care what you do with that drunk driver."

"The Jeep was stolen. Actually, the driver told me he was forced to steal it."

"Yeah, right," Lydia scoffed.

They were joined by another officer Lydia recalled seeing at the scene, standing behind the paramedics before the woman was loaded into the ambulance.

"Hi," the burly man said. "Here's your purse. Your vehicle's keys are in the side pocket."

Lydia felt her face pale. "Oh, no! I forgot all about my SUV! I think I left it running!"

"I pulled it over to the curb and locked it up. When we're finished here, I'll drive you back to pick it up." The officer smiled at her. "Or I can get someone to drive you home, if you don't feel up to driving."

Lydia considered her options while signing the statement she'd completed. "I'll be okay in a few minutes. Once I collect myself."

"Take your time. If I have any more questions for you I'll be back," the officer announced. "But I would like to discuss a few things with my partner before one of us drives you home."

"Okay," she muttered, smiling. "Thank you. I'll be here." Already she felt her eyes closing again. And she realized that, in all the commotion, she'd forgotten to call Warren.

Some time later, Lydia was startled awake by someone shaking her shoulder. "Miss?" Her eyes flew open and she glanced at the wall clock in the waiting area. An hour had passed.

"I'll drive you home now," the burly officer offered. If he'd told her his name, she couldn't recall it.

"That little nap helped. I'd prefer you take me to my SUV so I can drive myself home."

He nodded and they left the hospital.

Several minutes later, she thanked the officer for his kindness, then climbed into her vehicle, started the engine, and slowly headed to her mother's house on the reserve. She was so tired she could sleep for a week, but she'd never been so proud of herself.

# CHAPTER 14

*W*arren chopped vegetables for the banquet scheduled for later that afternoon. His hand healed more every day; maintaining the hand's former strength was imperative to his career. In his opinion, returning to work right away had been the best decision.

Nick charged into the kitchen. "Have you heard the news?"

Warren's head whipped up. "Oh, crap. Don't tell me the banquet was cancelled."

"Heck, no. Nothing like that. It's Lydia."

Warren's heart beat a little faster. "Did something happen?"

"I overheard a couple of the prep cooks talking about Lydia being out late last night. Also heard the words drunk driving and a car accident in the early hours this morning." Nick finished donning his chef's coat and then straightened his hat.

Warren stopped chopping and met Nick's eyes, fearing the reply but still needing to ask. "Was Lydia hurt in the accident?"

"They didn't mention anything."

Warren chopped a little more vigorously while attempting to wrap his mind around what he'd been told.

"The girl can be irresponsible," Nick chimed in. "I recall the time she plowed through the door, head down, clobbered you good."

"That was an unfortunate accident." Warren paused for a moment. But drunk driving? Why would any of her friends allow her to leave a bar with the intent to drive herself home after a night of drinking? Hell, no one working at the establishment should allow it. No way. Warren knew her. Lydia would *never* be involved in drunk driving.

Nick crossed his arms. "So I figure she caused the accident."

Before Warren could utter a word in Lydia's defense, a woman gasped, the sound coming from behind them.

Warren and Nick swung around.

Lydia stood in the doorway, a step ahead of the executive sous chef, her hands crushing the Stampede Catering apron she clasped.

Nick rested his hand on Warren's shoulder and whispered, "Oh, man. She overheard everything I said."

Lydia's eyes welled with tears which soon streamed down her cheeks. "Yeah, I heard every word. And, Warren Chamberland, you didn't say a single word in my defense. Or attempt to argue that Nick had to be wrong. Do you believe I would drink and drive? How could I have been so wrong about you?"

Nick stared at Warren. "Why didn't you tell me she was standing there?"

Lydia continued, "And to think I'd hoped you'd developed feelings for me!" She tossed the apron on the counter and met their boss's eyes. "I quit."

"Lydia, wait," Warren called as she stormed out of the kitchen.

Their boss glared at them.

"What did I say that wasn't the truth?" Nick blurted, hands on hips.

The boss related the true events that occurred the night before, as Lydia had informed him when she had arrived for work this morning. With each new revelation, Warren felt the blood drain from his face. He cringed, thinking about the ridiculous assumptions Lydia had overheard. He slumped onto a nearby stool while his boss finished relating the story, feeling sick to his stomach hearing the truth. How could he have listened to Nick's hearsay and not jumped in to defend the woman who meant so much to him?

Digesting the story of Lydia's brave efforts in saving the woman's life, Warren knew he alone was responsible for Lydia quitting the job she loved. He'd stood by listening to Nick when he should have immediately put a stop to the verbal insults. Why had he done it? What had he been waiting for?

Lydia's actions couldn't have been more heroic. Not only had she saved the pregnant woman's life, she'd guaranteed her unborn child's future also. Nick had totally misjudged her, and Warren had allowed it to happen. How would he ever make it up to her?

A lump formed in his throat. Would Lydia believe him when he told her he was about to defend her when she gasped and interrupted them? Would she believe he'd fallen in love with her?

Her boss would hire her back in a heartbeat; she was one of their best servers. But Warren's greatest fear was that Lydia wouldn't listen to any explanation he had to offer. Not one word he had to say. Including any apology.

# CHAPTER 15

Friday
Day eight of Stampede

*L*ydia hurried to answer the knock on her mother's back door.

"Grandfather! What are you doing here?" Lydia stepped aside, allowing him to enter the house. Had he heard what happened yesterday with Warren? She'd returned to the reserve after their encounter yesterday to avoid him.

"Your mother mentioned you had stayed here overnight again and that she made bannock this morning before she left for the Indian Village." He winked at Lydia, inhaling deeply. The scent of fresh-baked bannock hung in the air. "Thought I'd drop by for a taste. Make certain I approve."

Lydia playfully swatted her favorite elder's arm. "You know Mom makes the best bannock ever. Just admit you wanted some."

"Yes. Yes. And to see my favorite granddaughter." He seated himself while Lydia set a plate of bannock pieces, the butter dish and a jar of homemade strawberry jam on the kitchen table.

"Dig in," she encouraged him, pouring them both a cup of tea and then seating herself across from him.

They each sliced a still warm piece of bannock in half, buttered it and then spread on a liberal spoonful of jam.

"Diet food," Lydia teased, taking a big bite. She chewed and swallowed. "Remember the days when Mom arranged for you to watch me after school? You would have bannock and jam with a glass of milk waiting every time. And we'd sit at this table and share it, before I did my homework."

"I remember, my girl. You were a good student, always excellent marks." Grandfather smiled at her. "And we were all so proud of you."

"Yum…" Lydia murmured, licking her lips and then taking another big bite.

"Your mother is a very good cook," her grandfather added. "Almost as good as your grandmother was. I do miss her cooking."

"Nobody made venison stew and bannock better than Grandmother," Lydia said, smiling.

Her grandfather touched the side of his mouth and Lydia took the hint, wiping jam from her face. "Thank you," she whispered, the gesture a painful reminder of something Warren had done one morning when they'd shared a muffin at work. Before he'd shattered her feelings for him.

"What's wrong, my girl?"

She sighed heavily as her eyes welled with tears. She could never get anything past her intuitive grandfather.

"Something Warren did… or actually, something he didn't do," Lydia began, and then before she could stop herself, the entire story burst from her. Every accusation Nick spoke. Every assumption Nick made. And not a word from Warren to defend her.

Her grandfather sat, listening in silence. His expression unreadable. His thoughts his own.

When she finished spilling her tale, she sipped her tea and reached for another piece of bannock. Was Grandfather ashamed of her for not staying and defending herself? For storming out? She couldn't admit to him she'd quit her job.

Finally, he cleared his throat. "I look into your eyes. Witness your tears flowing, falling onto your cheeks. I see that this young man hurt you very much, my girl. The young man should have defended you against these accusations. He has made a mistake. Nobody is perfect though. And certainly, that young man isn't either, if he could stand by and listen to those assumptions about you."

Lydia leaned forward on her chair. "But what should I do, Grandfather? I liked him, until… If he were to offer me an apology, should I forgive him?"

"You will know when the time comes if forgiveness is the right thing to do."

Her grandfather had spoken so quietly that Lydia wasn't certain he realized he'd said the words aloud, but his comment made sense. She would know by the tone of Warren's voice and by the words he chose to convey his thoughts, whether or not the apology was sincerely meant.

Would she have the opportunity to make that decision? What if she never saw Warren again? She wouldn't be going to the commissary or catering buildings to work. But if they happened to cross paths on the grounds, could she bring herself to listen to him? For a man she'd fallen in love with to believe those things of her hurt beyond imagination.

LYDIA ACCOMPANIED her grandfather to the Stampede Park grounds where they were both scheduled to work at the Indian Village that afternoon. She enjoyed traveling into the city with him, in her SUV with the windows down and fresh air filling their lungs.

"You are a very good driver, Granddaughter. An admirable

talent in a busy city like Calgary. And you know all the shortcuts and streets to avoid during rush hour."

"Thank you. I love my new SUV." Lydia smiled as he patted her hand.

Parking on exhibition grounds was non-existent during Stampede and Lydia found a vacant spot to park her vehicle at a nearby C-train station. She purchased tickets for them and then they climbed aboard the next train to ride the remainder of the way to Stampede Park.

"I cannot recall the last time we rode the C-train." Bernard smiled, occupying the seat beside her. "At least, this is not as scary as riding the Sky Train inside the Stampede Grounds like you talked me into last year."

Lydia giggled. "You enjoyed it. And admit it. That's quite the view."

"Perhaps the view was nice. But I am not fond of heights, and Sky Train is one experience I do not feel compelled to repeat in this lifetime. I will leave that enjoyment to others."

They exited the train at the Victoria Park/Stampede station, moved through the station, briefly pausing for a minute so Bernard could catch his breath, and then exited. They strolled at a leisurely pace across the Stampede grounds. As they approached the midway, Lydia noticed Warren approaching them, staring intently at her.

"Is he your young man? Warren?" her grandfather whispered, pointing.

She met his eyes. "I don't want to hear a word he has to say." She turned on her heel.

"Lydia!" Warren called, running to catch up to her.

"I'm busy at Indian Village today. I don't have time to talk to you." She kept walking, never looking back.

∾

WARREN STOOD THERE, defeated. He couldn't blame Lydia for her rudeness. He'd known he'd hurt her deeply.

"My name is Bernard Crowchild. I'm Lydia's grandfather." The man stuck out his hand.

"I'm Warren Chamberland. It's good to meet you, sir. I haven't met any of Lydia's family." He shook hands with the old fellow.

Bernard stared at him. "Clean hair, neatly trimmed beard, pressed clothes, appearance tidy and well-kept. And handsome. I can understand why my granddaughter is attracted to you." He shrugged his shoulders. "Jumping to conclusions is perhaps your only fault."

Warren's mouth dropped open. A military commander couldn't offer a more in-depth inspection of him. Unfortunately, he doubted he'd won the old fellow's approval, especially where his granddaughter's heart was concerned. Perhaps he'd shattered any feelings of affection she might have developed for him with his inaction, failing to defend her against Nick's unfounded accusations.

"My granddaughter told me about the misunderstanding, and she remains very hurt by you. Only bad things happen when we make assumptions about other people." Bernard waved the young man over to a nearby picnic table.

Warren followed and took a seat across from him. "But that's the thing. I never thought Lydia would drive drunk. No way. But before I could defend her, she interrupted us. I should have spoken up immediately. I'm so sorry." He dragged his right hand through his hair. "I need to explain what happened to Lydia. Tell her I never for a moment thought those things about her. But she won't listen. I need to make things right again."

The old fellow crossed his arms over his chest and looked Warren in the eye, waiting for him to continue.

"I've heard the entire story. I learned the truth about the drunk driver. About Lydia's heroic actions saving two lives." Warren shifted forward on the seat. "I never doubted Lydia. I didn't. But I didn't speak up soon enough. She quit her job to avoid me."

Bernard's eyebrows rose and he scratched his chin. "She quit her job? That I hadn't heard."

"She tossed her apron onto the counter, announced she quit, and walked out." Warren glanced away, fighting to get his emotions under control. He blinked rapidly and took a deep breath. He couldn't love Lydia more and the misunderstanding between them was killing him.

Bernard uncrossed his arms and leaned forward. "Then perhaps you have your work cut out for you. I believe you care for my granddaughter. No matter what it takes, you should talk to her, explain how you feel and apologize."

"You believe there's still hope for us?"

"I do. If that is what you both truly want." Bernard stood. "Lydia is working in the Bannock Booth at Indian Village today. Perhaps you should drop by there."

Warren looked at his watch. "Darn it. I need to get back to work. But sooner or later I *will* talk to her. I love her, and one way or another, I need to make this right."

Bernard shook the young man's hand again. "Good luck to you, my boy. I hope things work out the way you want them to."

"Thank you, sir." Warren smiled and headed for work.

Did Lydia's grandfather like him? Especially after what he'd done? Her grandfather had encouraged him to make things right with her again. A first step, a positive step, toward her family accepting him in her life. Warren could only try to win back her heart. The alternative wasn't worth considering.

WARREN CHARGED into the BMO Centre and headed for the men's locker room inside the staff room. A minute later, he emerged wearing a clean chef's coat and poured himself a cup of coffee.

The executive chef joined him, pointing to a chair. "You got a minute?"

Warren's heartrate quickened. "Sure. I'm ten minutes early." He settled into one of the comfortable chairs across from the flat screen TV. The room was empty, except for the two of them. He hadn't expected this turn of events today. And he hadn't any idea what to expect.

"How's the hand doing?" His superior settled into a matching chair beside him and met his eyes.

"Good. Actually, really good. Pretty much off the painkillers now, except at night. And I've been taking my antibiotics and there's been absolutely no signs of infection." Warren kept his voice at an even level to disguise his apprehension.

The executive chef nodded. "One of the executive sous chefs reported that you returned to work a little prematurely."

Warren looked away for a second. The comment was a statement not a question; he couldn't deny it. "Yes, maybe a little earlier than the doctor intended. But I didn't have any problems because of it. And it wasn't the time of year to be missing work."

"I commend your dedication. And I'm glad it all worked out." The chef sipped his coffee. "Rumor has it you're intending to apply for some executive chef positions soon."

Warren swallowed hard. Hell, how had that news gotten back to him?

"Um… yes. I've learned so much here, but…"

"There is no where to go. Except for a lateral move." The chef nodded his head. "I completely understand. The two executive sous chefs and myself aren't going anywhere any time soon. For you to advance in your career, moving on makes perfect sense."

Warren couldn't believe what he was hearing.

The executive chef stood. "Let me know when you're ready to send out resumes. I'll provide you with a letter of recommendation. I don't mind giving someone like you a glowing report."

"Even after what I did?" Warren muttered.

The chef chuckled. "Accidents happen. People cut themselves. If I fired every chef who hurt himself, I'd be alone in the kitchen."

Warren leapt to his feet. "Thank you for your understanding, sir. I can't thank you enough for offering me a letter of recommendation."

"You've earned it. Your impeccable work ethic and the excellent work you've done here has been second to none. If I owned a high-end restaurant, I would hire you in a heartbeat. Kindly provide two weeks' notice when you've found your new position."

"I will." Warren smiled broadly. "Thank you, sir. I cannot tell you how much I've enjoyed working here. Learning from the best."

The chef nodded. "Thank you. And best of luck with your next endeavors."

Warren shook hands with his mentor and then watched him leave the room. He slumped back onto the chair he'd vacated, shaking his head in amazement. And he'd worried his superiors would learn about his plans and dismiss him before he'd found another job.

How did the old saying go? Fate moved in mysterious ways? Or was it God? Or something else altogether? Regardless, he'd polish his resume as soon as Stampede ended. The time had come to make his move. Too bad there weren't any openings at the Fairmont Palliser right now. But he'd noticed a couple of positions advertised online for executive chefs that would fit until his dream position opened. He'd willingly work under an executive chef for a year before expecting to run his own high-end restaurant. And with the recommendation from the executive chef at Stampede Catering, he couldn't wait to see where the future took him.

He glanced at the time on his cell.

"Providing you don't get canned for being late…" he muttered, dashing out of the room to start his shift.

# CHAPTER 16

Saturday
Second last day of Stampede

*W*arren had searched the entire Stampede grounds, desperately looking for Lydia. But with the huge grounds and so many venues to search, he could be doing this for days. With Stampede winding up tomorrow, he thought the grounds wouldn't be this busy late in the afternoon, compared to what he'd experienced the first few days. He'd been wrong. And he hadn't a clue as to what Lydia's schedule might include. Could she be working at the Indian Village again today? He'd initiated his search there, without seeing any trace of her. He'd sent her a few text messages which she'd ignored. And then he'd looked everywhere else. Still nothing.

He had plans with Nick later, but maybe the Indian Village was worth a second try.

He returned to the east side of the grounds and crossed the bridge over the Elbow River which meandered through the Stampede grounds. And there Lydia lingered beside the Bannock Booth. He'd found her. Finally.

She appeared to be waiting for someone, watching the entrance to the Indian Village. When she spotted him approaching, she clutched her large straw purse to her chest and turned to leave. No doubt she intended to avoid him entirely. He couldn't let that happen.

"Lydia, wait up," he called, jogging toward her.

She called over her shoulder, "I have nothing to say to you."

He caught up to her a few seconds later and gently grasped her arm. "Please stop. I need to apologize."

She brushed his hand away.

Warren was adamant he would talk to her. "Please. I don't want to cause a scene. Let me explain."

"All right. You have one minute." She leaned against a picnic table, appearing ready to bolt at any moment.

Warren took a deep breath. "Chef explained what happened. The truth. But I didn't need to hear a word of it. I never for a moment believed Nick's assumptions. But I didn't get the words out before you interrupted us."

Lydia stood arms crossed, silent.

"I shouldn't have waited. I should have cut him off when he first started in with his assumptions about you." Warren got down on one knee. "I'm begging you to please forgive me. You were right. I'm in love with you. I couldn't love you more."

Lydia's mouth dropped open.

"Get up," she whispered, grabbing him by the arm and hauling Warren to his feet. "People will think you're proposing."

"I am proposing."

She gaped at him.

"I'm proposing you forgive me." He winked at her, grinning.

"You're impossible. You know that, right?"

"Seriously, Lydia, I cannot tell you how sorry I am." He reached for her hand, entwined their fingers. "I would *never* think those things of you. Next time I will speak up immediately. I promise. I care too much about you to ever hurt you like that again."

"I love you, too," Lydia admitted "But when I overheard Nick's opinion of me, I was so hurt. And then you didn't say anything. I didn't know what to think."

"I know and I'm sorry." Warren wrapped her in his arms and held her tightly. He never wanted to let her out of his sight again. He lowered his head and kissed her deeply. She reached up on her tiptoes and ran her fingers through his hair. Man, he loved it when she did that… every time they kissed! The kiss lasted for several minutes, and he didn't care if they were making other people feel uncomfortable. He never wanted this moment to end.

Finally, she broke the kiss and heaved a sigh. "Okay, I forgive you," she whispered, her voice still breathy from the kiss they'd shared.

"Thank you." Warren looked deep into her eyes as his heartrate slowed a bit. "I love you so much. The thought of you never speaking to me again nearly killed me."

"Hey, Lydia," a young woman called from the Indian Village entrance.

Lydia waved to her friend, dropping her hands from Warren's shoulders.

Warren slipped his arm around Lydia's waist as the pretty blonde strode toward them.

"Sorry I'm late. I missed the C-train and then it was so crowded with concertgoers that I just made it here now." She smiled at Lydia.

"It's okay. We still have plenty of time." Lydia turned and smiled at Warren. "Emily, this is Warren Chamberland. Warren, this is my friend and roommate during the school year, Emily James."

"Hi. Pleased to meet you." Warren shook her hand.

"You, too," Emily offered. "So you're the chef I've heard so much about."

"Good things?"

"Well, until a few days ago…" Emily peeked over at Lydia.

"It's okay, Em. We've made up."

"What she means to say is she has kindly forgiven me," Warren clarified.

Emily's expression told him how surprised she was to hear it. Obviously, Lydia had shared with her friend what had happened. Would Emily as graciously accept that he and Lydia had made up as Lydia had accepted his apology? He didn't want to come between two good friends or force Lydia to choose between them.

"I'm happy she did forgive me, after I screwed up so badly," he added. "Tells you the kind of person she is."

"Lydia's the best," Emily agreed, smiling. "You would do well to remember that."

"Em!" Lydia exclaimed.

"He'd better treat you right or he'll have me to answer to."

Warren tightened his embrace with Lydia. "Oh, believe me. I've learned my lesson." He smiled at the contrast in the two women. Although identical in height and slim build, one was brunette with big brown eyes and the other a blue-eyed blonde with an extremely fair complexion. Complete opposites, but clearly the best of friends.

Emily rubbed her hands together. "Well, good. Now that that's settled, who's ready for a concert?"

"That's why you were waiting for her?" Warren gazed into Lydia's eyes.

"Yeah. We have tickets for Luke Bryan."

"So do we. I'm meeting Nick outside the Saddledome."

Lydia squeezed his arm. "We should all go together."

"Works for me," Emily added.

A half hour later, they met up with Nick outside Saddledome.

While walking into the building, the four of them compared their tickets. None of them had sprung for floor tickets, but miraculously, the four of them would be seated in the same area and only a few rows apart in the stands.

Nick and Warren had their heads together.

Emily poked Lydia's arm. "What do you suppose that's all about?"

"No idea." She shrugged.

Warren met Lydia's eyes. "We were wondering if you ladies would like to trade seating?"

The girls exchanged confused looks.

"I'll sit with Lydia," Warren ventured.

"And I'd love to sit with Emily," Nick chimed in.

Warren recalled Nick's weakness for blue-eyed blondes and Emily, every bit as cute and outgoing as Lydia, more than met his tastes.

A broad smile crossed Emily's face. "If it's okay with Lydia, I think that's an excellent idea."

Nick smiled at her. "I'm glad I suggested it."

"Fine with me," Lydia said, smiling. "And we're only four rows apart."

Tickets were exchanged between Warren and Emily and then she and Nick headed to their seats while Lydia and Warren found theirs.

"Hmm… I wonder if those two will start a relationship?" Lydia glanced over at Warren.

"Nick seems pretty interested in her." Warren watched his friend smiling from ear to ear, as he and Emily climbed the stands and settled into their seats. "She seems as nice a person as you are, and he really likes blonde, blue-eyed women."

"I'm happy for Emily, meeting a nice man. She's a little shy and I've never seen her so taken with a guy she just met." Lydia smiled. "I'm crossing my fingers for them."

The warmup act started playing, and Warren smiled at Lydia who was tapping her toe. He wondered what that fool Malcolm and his band were doing tonight? Thank goodness, Lydia hadn't agreed to his moronic idea to sing in his band. After saving the woman and unborn baby, Lydia intended to return to school in September, and he couldn't be happier about her decision.

When Luke Bryan took the stage, everyone leapt out of their seats, including Lydia and Warren. Amid the cheering and noise, Warren wrapped Lydia in his arms and kissed her. The music faded into the background as he deepened the kiss. He knew at that moment he would love her forever.

# CHAPTER 17

Sunday morning
Last day of Stampede

*L*ydia padded into the kitchen on bare feet, still in her pajamas, to make herself a cup of coffee. She yawned loudly. The concert had ended late and then they'd all gone for a midnight snack after. And after Warren dropped her off at the apartment, she realized her toothbrush and toiletries were still at her mom's place. Wide awake and still revved up from the exciting evening with her friends, she'd hopped into her SUV and driven out here.

"Four and a half hours sleep doesn't cut it," she muttered aloud, yawning again.

She stuck a pod in the Keurig and waited for her cup of wakeup to brew. She removed her coffee mug from the brewing stand and wandered back into the living room. A knock on the door distracted her from her thoughts, and she set her mug on the coffee table and strode to the front door.

"Grandfather! Hi! I didn't know you were coming over." Lydia waited until he'd stepped inside and then hugged him warmly.

Her grandfather wandered into the living room and settled himself in the recliner by the fireplace. "We haven't talked for a few days."

"Would you like a cup of coffee?" Lydia settled onto the sofa, tucking her feet under her.

"No, thank you, my girl." Grandfather smiled. "I thought perhaps we could talk about your young man, the chef. I like him."

Lydia reached for the mug of coffee. "You've met Warren?" She bobbed her head when she realized he would have. "That day I refused to talk to him. What did he say to you?"

"Many things. Interesting words. He cares for you very much," Grandfather reported. "And he is very sorry for what he said to you, doubting you. He reminds me of your father. I believe he is a good man, my girl."

Lydia set the mug down, leapt off the sofa, and dropped to her knees beside the recliner. Her grandfather leaned forward and she hugged him tightly. "There is no one on earth whose opinion I value more than yours. Warren and I made up last night. I accepted his apology. Warren told me he loves me. And I love him, too," she admitted.

Grandfather smiled. "This news does not surprise me."

Lydia laughed. She could never get anything past this intuitive old man. "We attended the concert with Emily and his friend, Nick. He also apologized for his wrongful assumptions. Said he'd learned his lesson about listening in on conversations."

Grandfather leaned back, crossing his arms over his chest. "So, you have decided that there is a future for you with Warren."

"I hope so. Part of my future anyway." Lydia rose to her feet. "The outcome from the accident solidified in my mind that nursing was my destiny. I'm returning to university in September. And I'm going to hang in there and finish my degree, then become an RN."

"You sound determined, my girl. I like hearing these words."

"Thank you. I mean it, Grandfather. I'm going to do it. Saddle my dream of becoming a nurse and then ride that dream to completion." Lydia smiled, recalling the words of wisdom that Warren had shared with her.

Her grandfather laughed. "My, my, my. I love that."

"Words of wisdom from Warren's father," Lydia explained.

"A wise man. I would like to meet him someday."

Lydia reached for his hand. "I'm looking forward to meeting Warren's family some day, also."

She meant every word, and she'd decided that nursing and Warren were her future. And after the wonderful time they'd shared together last night, socializing with their best friends, nothing seemed impossible to her.

"I have somewhere I should be, Grandfather." Lydia kissed his cheek. "I'm going to surprise Warren."

"Tell him I said hello." Her grandfather hefted himself out of the recliner and snagged her mug off the coffee table. He took a sip. "Good coffee."

Lydia threw her head back and laughed. "Help yourself to my coffee. I haven't time to finish it." She winked at him and hurried down the hallway to shower and change into clothes.

## CHAPTER 18

*W*arren rolled over in bed and grabbed his cell phone off the nightstand, noticing it was already eight o'clock. "Hello."

"Warren, it's Mom."

He sat bolt upright in bed, knowing his mother wouldn't be calling this early in the morning if it wasn't important. He grimaced with the pain in his head. Shouldn't have gotten into those shooters as well as the beer after the concert.

"What's wrong?"

"There was…an accident…"

"Dad?" Warren dragged his hand through his hair, wishing he could avoid the rest of this conversation. A bad feeling hit him like a ton of bricks.

"Yes… and…and your brother." His mother was sobbing, and he could barely understand her.

"Both of them?" Bile rose into his throat and he swallowed hard. "What happened?"

"They decided to fly to Calgary, to take in the Stampede for the final day."

"And?" Warren encouraged her to continue.

"The Cessna crashed shortly after takeoff here on the ranch." His mother sobbed, her words garbled. "Just fell out of the sky not long after takeoff. STARS Air Ambulance arrived within what seemed like minutes and air-lifted them to the Foothills Hospital."

Warren sat on the edge of the bed, stunned.

"I'm not certain either of them will make it," his mother wailed. "I called Karen and she's leaving the boys with a neighbor."

"You're on the way into the city?"

"Jerry Wright saw it happen and came tearing over here in his pickup. He's driving me and your sister-in-law into Calgary. Can you get to the hospital? See if... if they're still alive?"

"Yeah, Mom. Thank God for great neighbors." Warren hung up.

Just then he heard a loud knock on his apartment door.

Slipping into a pair of sweatpants, he whipped the door open. "This isn't a good time to—"

"Surprise!" Lydia beamed at him, dressed in faded jeans and a short-sleeved white hoodie, holding a to-go tray of coffees and a bag from Tim Hortons.

Warren shook his head. "I can't..."

"What's wrong? I can tell by your face something happened." Lydia stepped into the apartment closing the door behind her. "Is it your hand? Is there an infection?"

"It's not me, but I need to get to Foothills Hospital," Warren muttered.

"What happened?" Lydia searched his face. "Is it Nick?"

Warren shook his head and raced down the hallway. "My father and brother. Plane crash at the ranch."

Lydia frowned. "Someone's plane crash-landed on your ranch?" she called.

"Our plane. Our Cessna crashed on takeoff for some reason." Warren dashed out of the bedroom, dressed in jeans and a shirt. He whipped open the closet door and slipped his feet into a pair of sandals. "Mom called. STARS flew them to Foothills. Mom and my sister-in-law are on the way into the city from High River, but I need to go to the hospital and see how bad it was. See if they…survived."

Lydia set the coffees down. "I'll drive you. Let's go."

"Bring the coffee. I'll need it," Warren said, opening the apartment's door.

Lydia grabbed the coffee tray and dashed out the door. A few minutes later, they were headed toward Foothills in her SUV.

"I don't know how this could happen," Warren mumbled, gulping the warm coffee while Lydia drove. "We've always kept the plane well-maintained, precisely so something like this wouldn't happen."

"Who was flying?"

Warren wracked his brain. "Mom didn't say. But all of us fly except for her."

"You're a pilot?" Lydia blurted.

Warren nodded. "And Dad and Blaine are both excellent pilots also. Neither of them would fly if they suspected there was a problem with the plane."

Lydia turned onto 16th Avenue heading west. "Well, let's not expect the worst. We'll know soon enough."

"Can't you drive any faster?"

"Warren, these posted speed limits aren't simply a suggestion." Lydia scolded him. "I'm not getting into an accident, okay?"

"Sorry. This uncertainty is making me a little crazy." Warren stared out the passenger side window, the scenery a blur. His dad and brother couldn't die. Who would carry on if they didn't survive this?

Lydia parked and together they hurried into the hospital where Warren strode toward the main entrance desk.

"Can someone tell me the condition of Dave Chamberland and Blaine Chamberland? They came in by STARS after a small plane crash."

"Who are you?" the nurse demanded.

"Son and brother." Warren handed her his driver's license.

The nurse examined it closely, then stared at the screen on her computer. Warren recited his father's and brother's full names, their dates of birth, and their address in High River. The information must be in their records. Everyone in the entire family had been admitted to Foothills at one time or another, over the years.

"Okay. Let me check on their condition," the nurse said, punching more keys on her computer keyboard and then she grabbed the phone. "David Chamberland is scheduled for surgery. Let me check on the other gentleman."

*Let them be okay.*

For several minutes, Warren paced the floor while Lydia slumped in a chair. At least his dad was alive, if he'd been scheduled for surgery. But what about Blaine? If anything happened to him, his sister-in-law would be devastated. And his sons would lose their father.

Warren strode to the desk. "Dammit, what's taking so long?"

The nurse looked up; he'd interrupted her conversation on the phone.

"Sorry," Warren muttered. "Let me know when you hear something."

The nurse nodded her head.

Warren dragged his right hand through his hair. "Oh crap." He yanked his cell phone out of his pocket and called his boss at work.

"Hey, I'm sorry I forgot to call sooner. My dad and brother were in a small plane crash. I'm at the Foothills. I can't leave my mom and sister-in-law to face this alone," Warren blurted.

"No problem. Stampede is winding down. We can spare you today," his boss replied immediately.

"Thanks for understanding." Warren sighed.

"Call again tomorrow if you're unable to come in. Good luck to your family."

"Thanks. I appreciate your compassion. And I won't forget to call again tomorrow." Warren ended the call and stuffed the phone in his pocket.

Just then his mother and Karen stepped through the entrance doors and hurried to his side.

Warren gaped. Was he seeing things? "Mom, Karen, how did you get here so fast?"

"Ralph Waters heard about the crash. He called Jerry and insisted he drive us to his place. Ralph flew us here." His mother's face paled. "Took every bit of my strength to climb into that plane."

Karen chimed in, "Ralph rented a car at the Calgary airport and then drove us here."

"That drive from the airport took more years off my life than the plane trip did. The man's a maniac." His mother wrung her hands as she spoke.

"But we're here now in one piece," Karen stated, clasping his mother's hand. "Ralph said to call his cell when we're ready to return home."

Lydia appeared at Warren's side and reached for his hand. "This is Lydia Simpson-Crowchild." Warren introduced everyone.

Lydia nodded. "Hi."

"Have you heard anything?" Karen blurted.

Warren shook his head. "Not much. Dad's scheduled for surgery. Nothing yet on Blaine."

His mother's eyes filled with tears. "We need to talk to someone."

Warren knew his mother was trying to remain strong and in control. But being in the dark about what was happening to her husband and other son would be killing her inside. "I'll ask the nurse again." He strode over to the desk and made inquiries.

"The surgeon will be out to talk to you about your father shortly," the nurse informed him. "I'm still waiting to hear about the other man."

"Thank you." Warren walked to his mother's side.

Karen paced, tears trickling from her eyes.

Lydia was consoling his mother, their arms wrapped around each other. How had he been so lucky to win the heart of such a wonderful young woman. He truly loved Lydia, and seeing her with his mother was evidence the girl was someone he wanted in his life always.

Lydia stepped back. "What's the word?"

Warren hugged his mother. "Dad's surgeon should be here shortly. The nurse is still looking for an update on Blaine."

Tear-filled eyes met his. "Thank you for checking," his mother whispered.

Karen's face paled and she sobbed in earnest.

"Just because we haven't heard anything about Blaine yet, doesn't mean it will be bad news," Warren told his sister-in-law. Not certain he believed his own pep talk, Warren wrapped his arms around Karen until she'd gotten her tears under control. And then he joined her, pacing the waiting area.

The electric doors slid open and a middle-aged man in green scrubs strode into the waiting area. Clean-shaven, trim and fit, the man carried a tablet in his hands.

"I'm Dr. Gibson. Someone is here for David Chamberland?"

Warren's mother rushed forward. "He's my husband!"

Warren, Karen and Lydia hurried over to her side and Warren took her hand.

"Are you all family?"

"Yes, Dr. Gibson!" Warren blurted before anyone else replied. "What can you tell us?"

"Mrs. Chamberland, your husband has been evaluated and he requires surgery to relieve pressure on his back. There are major issues with his spine. The spinal cord might be severed, but we won't be certain how extensive the damage until the swelling goes down. The spine might only be crushed but I'm not wagering any guesses. The x-rays should tell us more."

"Will he live?" his mother whispered.

"If there are no occurrences during surgery, I'm optimistic he'll be fine. Might be wheelchair-bound, but we'll worry about that when the time comes." Dr. Gibson touched his mother's hand. "His heart is strong and he's complaining to the nurses. All good signs."

His mother smiled weakly. "Tell my husband to behave himself. And that I'll be waiting to see him after his surgery."

The doctor nodded.

"What about my husband? Blaine Chamberland?" Karen whispered.

"Another doctor is still evaluating him." Dr. Gibson nodded. "Dr. Mitchell will send word as soon as he knows something conclusive."

Karen nodded, tears slipping down her cheeks.

"Now, the paperwork authorizing surgery is ready for signing." The surgeon headed toward the sliding doors.

"Thank you," Warren called, steering his mother and Karen toward the desk.

While the paperwork was being handled, Warren wandered off to the side. This is exactly what he deserved. Bragging to everyone, including Lydia, that absolutely *nothing* would keep him from achieving his goal. All that was needed was determination and hard work, he'd said. Buckle down and he'd become an executive chef employed at his dream job, he'd insisted. All of his boasting had slapped him in the face.

In an instant, Fate had stepped in where she had no business being, possibly ending the life of his father and his brother and totally derailing his big plans!

# CHAPTER 19

*L*ydia took a break from waiting with Warren, Karen and his mother. The surgeon hadn't given them much of a report, except to say both men were still alive and being evaluated. Mrs. Chamberland had signed all the paperwork for Warren's dad, and Karen signed them for her husband. Last she'd heard, David Chamberland's surgery was underway.

Now they waited.

Lydia bought herself a coffee from a vending machine and then paced the hallways, nerves on edge. And this wasn't even her family. She couldn't say that aloud, recalling Warren's little white lie. But she'd seen that haunted look in the eyes of relatives before, waiting for news that seemed would never come. She understood what Warren and his family were going through.

*Please let it be good news.*

"Ms. Simpson-Crowchild."

Hearing her name called, Lydia turned and smiled at the police officer she'd met when he took her statement the night of the accident on Crowchild Trail.

"Hi, I remember you." Lydia greeted the officer who was dressed in uniform and obviously on duty.

"I had a couple more questions for Mrs. Robertson." The officer stood beside Lydia. "How are you doing?"

"Fine," she offered. "How's Mrs. Robertson?"

"She's doing well. I'm happy to hear you are, too." The officer crossed his arms over his chest. "The drunk driver was arrested and gave his statement."

"I bet he had a great story to tell," she scoffed.

The officer nodded. "My thoughts, too, at the time. But we learned he's a street kid, released from the foster system a few months ago. He's been running with a bad crowd."

"Getting drunk and stealing cars."

"He's looking at jail time. But I hope he also gets some help and straightens himself out. The kid needs someone to give him a break."

"I guess so," Lydia muttered, not completely convinced. "The kid needs to learn a lesson, and initially I wanted him to rot in jail. But incarceration at a young age could turn him into a career criminal. I've seen it happen with a couple of the boys I grew up with. Maybe the judge will be lenient."

"I do have a message for you. From the kid."

"Are you serious?"

"He said to tell the woman thank you for saving the pregnant lady's life. Or he'd be facing a murder charge, not drunk driving, car theft and reckless endangerment." The officer's eyebrows rose. "Apparently, his single-parent mother was an alcoholic. When she died, he was placed into the foster system. He intends to quit drinking, and he sounds sincerely remorseful."

Lydia nodded. "Well, that's something. Tell him he can thank me by getting his act together."

"I'll tell him that. Mrs. Robertson mentioned she'd like to talk to the woman who saved her. I would need your permission to give her your cell number. Or you could drop by and visit her." He wrote down the room number and handed her the slip of paper while telling her the directions to the location.

"I…I guess I could visit and see how she's doing," Lydia offered.

"I'm certain she'd be happy to see you." The officer smiled. "Take care, miss. I've got to go."

"Nice talking to you again." Lydia watched him disappear into the elevator.

She paused for a moment and then moved toward the elevator herself.

A couple days ago, Lydia hadn't relished the thought of returning to the place that held conflicting memories for her. Some so horrible; others causing moments of elation. But she'd come anyway and located the RN who gave her the scrubs that night. She'd returned them laundered, thanking the nurse again for her kindness and consideration.

Now, here she was, facing memories of that night again. She strode to the nurses' desk to ask directions to Sharon Robertson's room. The nurse assigned to Sharon accompanied her down the hallway where she knocked lightly on her door.

"Come in," a woman called.

"You have a visitor." The nurse accompanied Lydia into the room.

"Hello." The woman lay in the hospital bed, frowning.

"I'm Lydia." The young mother-to-be wouldn't recognize her. "You were unconscious the entire time I was with you."

"Lydia! If you're not my guardian angel, you'll most certainly do until she shows up," Sharon teased, smiling. Being quite pregnant and still recovering from surgery, she required the nurse's assistance to sit up in the bed.

"Come sit with me, Lydia." Sharon patted the side of the narrow hospital bed. She wore a floral cotton maternity nightgown, probably one of her own. A pair of fluffy pink slippers covered her feet. A sheet had been thrown loosely across her middle, covering her legs and her injury.

Lydia dragged the visitor chair closer. "This will work, Mrs. Robertson."

"Please, call me Sharon."

"Okay."

The woman smiled. "Due to your quick-thinking, you saved my life. I cannot tell you how thankful I am." Sharon's eyes filled with tears as she rubbed her huge tummy. "And my baby's life, too."

"You're…you're welcome," Lydia stammered, close to tears. She'd promised herself she wouldn't cry anymore at a patient's bedside. But it was so hard to wrangle her emotions under control.

"That stupid vase. Had you wondered where the shard of glass came from? My husband bought me flowers for my birthday, the night we had dinner at his mother's house. She lent me one of her beautiful pinwheel crystal vases and after the flowers died, I washed the vase and left it in the car to return it when I next saw her."

Lydia shook her head. How could she ever forget the jagged shard of glass that caused the near-fatal wound. "Unfortunate timing. You couldn't have known."

Tears slipped down Sharon's cheeks. "I'm eight months along. I've already suffered two miscarriages, and my doctor kept encouraging me to try again. Now, this baby is so close to full-term."

Lydia gave up trying to remain dry-eyed, feeling wetness on her own cheeks. "I'm so happy I saved you both."

"If it hadn't been for your quick-thinking." Sharon swiped at her tears. "An older couple popped in to visit me yesterday. Gerry and Marianne. They told me everything you did. How efficient you were. How professional and knowledgeable."

Lydia recalled the man who gave her his tie for the tourniquet. "Did he mention I ruined one of his neckties?" she asked, smiling.

Sharon nodded.

"Nice gray-patterned one," Lydia added. "Might have cost a fortune."

Sharon laughed through her tears. "I'll see to it my husband buys him a new one."

"That would be kind of you."

Sharon wiped her eyes with the corner of the sheet. "It feels good to laugh."

Lydia nodded in agreement. "How are you feeling?"

"Good. The surgery to repair my leg went well. The doctor told me that the tests indicate I should still carry the baby to full term."

Lydia reached over and touched her hand. "That's the best news yet."

"Of course, nothing is for sure. And this was always considered a high-risk pregnancy because of my history."

"But the test results sound positive?"

"Yes, but my doctor insists I avoid crystal vases and stress." Sharon laughed and waved her hand around. "So, this isn't the Hilton or Palliser, but it's home until I go into labor. My doctor is not taking any chances by sending me home."

Lydia shifted in her chair. "If you don't mind me asking, what on earth were you doing out in your car at two o'clock in the morning?"

"You would have to ask." Sharon's face reddened. "So ridiculous, now that I think about it."

Lydia waited for the explanation.

"Milk," she whispered.

"Milk?"

"I couldn't sleep. So I snuck out of bed, not wanting to wake my husband." Sharon's fingers played with the edge of the blanket on the bed while she spoke. "I wanted a glass of milk. But we were out. So I figured I'd pick some up at the 24-hour corner store. Wouldn't take more than a few minutes. We'd need some for breakfast anyway. I must have been preoccupied with my thoughts since I missed the turn-off, so I continued down Crowchild intending to turn off and circle back."

Lydia leaned forward in her seat.

"And then another vehicle clipped my car. I remember the car spinning out of control and having no hope of stopping it. I remember another car hitting me and closing my eyes. Then everything went black." Sharon shrugged. "Even now I don't remember the impact. Apparently, it was a horrible collision."

"It happened in front of me, as if in slow motion. And there wasn't a thing I could do about it." Lydia shook her head. "I've never felt so powerless."

"But you knew what to do." Sharon smiled. "My husband and I can never thank you enough."

"Just give birth to a healthy baby and invite me to come see him," Lydia suggested.

"*That* I intend to do." Sharon smiled. "I wish this was a girl so I could call her Lydia. Such a beautiful name."

Lydia laughed. "That's so nice of you. But I don't imagine your husband wants a son called Lydia. So, you'd best wait for a baby girl."

"That's probably for the best," Sharon agreed, smiling.

Lydia exchanged cell phone numbers with Sharon.

"I want my son to know the woman who saved his life and his mother's life. We are going to stay in touch," Sharon promised.

Lydia teared up. "I'd like that, too."

"I'd heard that you're a nursing student." Sharon smiled. "I know you'll save many more lives."

Lydia leaned forward in her chair. "Since school finished, I've been doubting whether or not I should become a nurse," she confided. "I spent a great deal of time crying at bedsides during my practicum. I'd convinced myself I was too soft-hearted. Too emotional."

"Don't doubt your calling. You were born to be a nurse." Sharon gripped her hand. "Promise me you'll complete your training. You should spend your entire career saving lives. Like you saved mine."

Lydia nodded. "I promise." She knew now that Sharon was right. As her mother had been when she'd encouraged Lydia to follow in her footsteps. Talking with the grateful mother-to-be solidified Lydia's conviction.

She wanted to be a nurse.

She needed to be a nurse.

Minutes later, after saying her goodbyes to Sharon, Lydia headed to where Warren and his family waited, hoping that they'd heard good news by now. "I'm going to be the best nurse I can be," she vowed.

～

WARREN WELCOMED Lydia back with a kiss. "Where did you disappear to?"

"I needed to walk for a while, and I visited Sharon, the woman in the accident."

"How's she doing?"

"Pretty good actually." Lydia smiled at him. "I bought a coffee out of a vending machine, intending to bring some for everyone. It didn't taste the best."

"Just as well, we're Tim Hortons-or-nothing kind of people," Warren explained.

"Me, too. Did you learn anything?" Lydia met his eyes, looking hopeful.

Warren took her hand and led her down the hallway. "We finally convinced Mom to sit and rest so I don't want to disturb her."

Lydia nodded.

Warren leaned against the wall. "They did surgery on Dad to relieve pressure on his back. No further updates on him. He could spend the rest of his life in a wheelchair, but we'll know more later." Warren glanced away for a moment, blinking. "But he's alive," he whispered.

"Thank goodness for that." Lydia touched his arm. "What about your brother?"

"Blaine lost a lot of blood before the paramedics arrived.

Multiple internal injuries. His heart stopped once in the air ambulance." Warren paused for a moment, taking a deep breath.

"He's alive, too," Lydia reminded him.

"Yeah, you're right. He was stable enough for surgery. They removed his spleen, but we haven't received another update for a while." Warren hugged Lydia, needing her warmth. "Mom is afraid Blaine won't make it. Karen is a wreck, especially hearing the words 'multiple internal injuries'."

Lydia slipped out of his arms and strode toward the waiting area.

"Karen?" she whispered.

Warren's sister-in-law met her eyes.

Lydia seated herself beside Karen and took her hand. "Don't fear the worst." She spoke softly so as not to disturb Warren's mother on a nearby chair. "Internal injuries could mean anything. Warren told me Blaine had his spleen removed but people can live trouble-free without it. Blaine's going to be fine."

Karen forced a smile. "Thank you. Warren told us you're training to be a nurse."

Lydia nodded.

"I appreciate your words of encouragement. I'll try not to dwell on possible worst case scenarios." Karen squeezed Lydia's hand.

Lydia smiled. "Think positive thoughts."

"Thank you," Karen whispered, crossing her fingers.

Warren's thoughts were a jumble. He tuned out the rest of the conversation between Lydia and Karen. Would Blaine survive this? Could his brother take over the ranch? Obviously, his father wouldn't be capable of running a ranch from a wheelchair. Well, perhaps the paperwork end of it. Which would be absolute hell on a hands-on kind of guy like his dad. But paperwork and decision-making were better than nothing. Was there hope that both of them would survive the crash?

## CHAPTER 20

Sunday evening
Last day of Stampede

*L*ydia startled awake. She must have dozed off in the waiting room chair. Warren sat in the chair beside her, gazing at the ceiling.

"How long was I asleep?" She stretched her back and rotated her neck.

"A couple hours. It's a little past six o'clock."

"Have you heard anything new about Blaine?" She reached for Warren's hand.

"Nothing," Warren mumbled, sounding half-asleep. "I think Dad's been assigned a room. His surgery went well. We haven't heard anything yet about Blaine. I assume he's still in surgery."

"I guess no news is still good news." Lydia noticed Karen sitting in a chair opposite hers, and his mother was pacing again, farther down the hallway.

"Everything depends on the outcome today." Warren reached for her hand. "Whether my brother recovers."

"Your sister will be devastated if…" Lydia couldn't finish the thought, having seen how close-knit Warren's family was.

"It's my fault." Warren shook his head.

Lydia's mouth dropped open. "How could that plane crash be your fault?"

"Well, maybe not the crash." Warren shifted in the chair. "But I've been so arrogant about my aspirations, my goals, my future. Knowing exactly what I wanted and bragging that *nothing* would stop me from achieving my dream of being an executive chef at my dream job."

She tilted her head. "I don't understand what you mean."

"All that changed in a heartbeat. In the few seconds it took for the Cessna to fall out of the sky." Warren dragged his hand through his hair. "Dad isn't capable of working the ranch now. And if Blaine doesn't survive, Mom will insist I take over. Fate is putting me in my place."

"Would that be so bad? Lots of guys would jump at the chance to operate a ranch." Lydia moved closer to him. "Some of my cousins on the reserve raise and breed horses and they love the Western lifestyle."

"Yeah, well, not me. I couldn't wait to leave and take culinary training." Warren stood and started pacing. "I hated working in every imaginable weather condition: blinding snow, freezing rain, blazing sun. Expected to be up early and work until dark seven days a week. Delivering calves in the middle of the night. Doctoring ailing horses at all hours. Mending fences, building corrals. Never able to say everything is done now, always more that needed doing, often costing more money than budgeted for. Bankers know ranchers by their first names. And the name of the rancher's wife and his kids and the dog. Get a loan paid off and you'll probably need another one. I hated everything about the ranch and the entire lifestyle."

"Even the horses? The cows?"

Warren shook his head and returned to his chair. "I love

animals as much as anyone. Just not 24/7. But my brother was always better with the horses than me. And he loved working with the cattle, even delivering a calf at two in the morning."

"But why become a chef?"

"I helped Mom in the kitchen, since she didn't have any daughters." Warren smiled at the memories. "I loved creating my own masterpieces for the holidays, working in the garden during the summer months with Mom, growing our own veggies and fruits, making jams, and preserving and canning what we harvested. Once my ranch chores were done, I'd spend every waking moment in the kitchen."

"I bet you were a big help for your mom. She must have appreciated it."

"Of course, she did. But my dad and brother laughed and teased me. Suzy Homemaker was my brother's favorite name for me, especially in high school whenever I signed up for cooking courses while he chose things like woodworking. But I didn't care. I knew what I enjoyed. And Dad and Blaine were always so close, sharing so many of the same interests, sometimes I felt like the spare son."

"So you decided becoming a chef was your destiny and you left the ranch."

"Never looked back for a moment, figuring nothing could stop me. And now this."

"Don't expect the worst."

"I can't help it. How can I turn my back on the family, Lydia? If something happens, it would kill Mom if I didn't step up. Take over the ranch that has been in Dad's family for five generations."

"Nothing is for certain yet." Lydia met his eyes. "Warren, you're a good man and I know you'll do the right thing. If it ever comes to that."

"I've thought about this a lot today. There's nothing saying I have to run the ranch, day-to-day. Completely hands-on. I'll hire a manager who knows what he's doing. I'll become an executive chef, but also hire people to operate the ranch under my leadership. Anything is possible with the right planning and manpower."

"You think so?"

"I know so, and I'm going to stop worrying until we learn something." Warren looked up, hearing footsteps approaching. His mother hurried toward them, tears streaming down her cheeks. "Crap, something happened." He leapt off the chair and rushed to her, enveloping her in his arms. "What happened, Mom? Was it Blaine? He didn't make it?"

Lydia covered her mouth with her hand. *No. Please, no.*

Now, his mother was crying and smiling at the same time. "Blaine came through the surgery with flying colors. The surgeon repaired all the damage. The next twenty-four hours will tell us more, but the doctor sounded so confident he'll make a full recovery."

"Blaine is going to be all right?" Warren whispered.

"Yes," his mother said, hugging Karen who'd leapt off her chair and followed Warren.

Soon, both women were crying.

Lydia blinked back her own tears.

"You're so soft-hearted," Warren whispered. "You don't know Blaine and you're crying, too."

Lydia swatted his arm. "Never mind."

Warren laughed and wrapped her in his arms.

"We're going to see your brother," his mother called and she and Karen disappeared down the hallway.

"Now, you see? All that worrying for nothing," Lydia teased him, holding him tight.

Warren heaved a sigh. "At least the outcome sounds optimistic. But I would have done it for Mom."

"I know you would have." Lydia nodded. "Seeing Sharon Robertson's life hang in a balance the other night showed me how vulnerable we all are to situations that are none of our own doing.

But we have to live every day like it could be our last. And not worry about what Fate has in store for us."

"You're right." Warren slipped out of her arms and met her eyes.

"Be a good person. Live life to its fullest. Appreciate the people in your life…"

"Love one another," Warren chimed in.

Lydia smiled. "I do love you. So much."

"I love you, too." Warren kissed her softly.

"Then we should get on with life and let the future take care of itself." She reached for his good hand and tugged him toward the elevator. "Starting with a bite to eat."

"I'm starving." Warren nibbled on her ear as they waited for the elevator to arrive. "And not only for food."

Lydia smiled at him. "Naughty, naughty."

"I can be naughty. If you insist," Warren whispered in her ear.

"We could get takeout?"

Warren laughed. "Best offer I've had in ages."

"I love you." Lydia kissed him. "And whether you're a chef or a rancher, nothing will change that."

# CHAPTER 21

Saturday morning after Stampede

Shortly before eleven o'clock, Lydia peeked into the hospital room through the open doorway, noticing the colorful patchwork quilt on the narrow bed. Flowers lined the windowsill and covered a small table as well.

"Hello?" she ventured, knocking softly on the door.

A familiar female voice called, "Come in."

Lydia hesitated for a moment. Should she have decided to pop in unannounced? She'd finished visiting with Sharon Robertson for over an hour and while she waited for the elevator, she realized she knew other patients in the Foothills Hospital. On the spur of the moment, she'd decided to check on Warren's father and brother, starting with his dad.

Warren's mother popped her head around the corner. "Lydia! Come in, dear. Come in."

Lydia smiled and slowly entered the room. A gray-haired man was lying back against several pillows, his hair in slight disarray as if he'd just woken from a nap. He wore a plain white t-shirt and a pair of slightly faded Calgary Flames pajama bottoms. A frown appeared on his face when he spotted her.

"This is Warren's girlfriend, dear. Don't you remember him talking about Lydia?" Mrs. Chamberland patted her husband's arm as she spoke.

A broad smile blossomed immediately, his tanned face evidence of his hands-on work on the family ranch. "Hello, Lydia," he said. "Pleased to meet you."

"Hello, Mr. Chamberland. It's so nice to meet you, too. How are you feeling?" Lydia smiled.

"Like I've been knocked about pretty good." He sat, arms crossed over his chest. "Sitting in this damn hospital when I should be checking on the ranch, but they won't let me have my cell phone."

"Now, dear, keep your spirits up. Young Benny and Matt are looking after the ranch. And Jerry drops over every night to check up on them." His wife scolded him. "Besides, tests today showed evidence that David has some feeling in his legs. Not a lot, mind you, but some. The doctors believe his spine was bruised but not crushed as previously thought. We're hopeful there wasn't as much spinal damage as we initially feared."

"That's wonderful news."

Mr. Chamberland patted his wife's hand. "Hell, doesn't mean I'll walk someday, but I guess it's a start."

Lydia gazed around the room. "You must have dozens of friends, judging by all these lovely flowers."

"Who ever heard of buying flowers for a man? It's ridiculous," Mr. Chamberland complained. "Flowers are meant for ladies."

"Now, dear. What would you have preferred people buy you?" his wife inquired.

"Could have bought a bottle of scotch instead." The deeply-tanned, broad-shouldered rancher's expression brought a smile to his wife's face.

"Stop sulking, David." His wife shook her head. "Patients can't have alcohol in the hospital, dear."

"Would have just taken it home."

Mrs. Chamberland ignored her husband's comment. "Lydia, it's so nice of you to drop by. Warren texted me a couple minutes ago. He's on his way up in the elevator."

"Oh, maybe I should go then," Lydia ventured.

"Nonsense. You're welcome here, too." Mrs. Chamberland smiled.

Warren strolled into the room. "Hi, Mom," he said, kissing her cheek." He gazed toward his father's bed and spotted Lydia standing there. She offered him a smile; he looked shocked to see her. "Hi, Dad. Lydia, you're here, too?"

"She just arrived. Such a pleasant surprise," his mother chimed in.

He gave Lydia a peck on the lips. "Hi, beautiful."

"Hi." She hugged his left arm.

Warren leaned forward and shook his father's hand. "How are you feeling, Dad?"

"Good as can be expected, I guess," his father muttered. "Food's pretty good. Better than I figured."

"Speaking of food… Warren is taking me to dinner tonight at the Calgary Tower," Lydia ventured, a delaying tactic until she'd decided how she should broach the subject that brought her here.

"That sounds lovely." Mrs. Chamberland met her husband's eyes. "We've enjoyed so many pleasant meals there over the years, haven't we, dear?"

Mr. Chamberland nodded. "Yes, we did. Excellent food. You kids will enjoy it."

Warren smiled. "Thanks, Dad. I'm sure we will."

"I can't wait. I'm certain it will be a lot of fun. But I do have a purpose for being here. I hope you won't mind, and hospitals allow this now." Lydia took a deep breath. "I would like to perform a smudging ceremony for you, Mr. Chamberland. If you will permit it." She met his eyes, uncertain if he would understand her request.

Mr. Chamberland smiled for the first time since she'd entered his room. "Little girl, I need all the help I can get. You go right ahead and do your ceremony."

Lydia felt herself beaming. "Thank you." She set her large straw bag on the foot of his bed and dug out her materials: abalone shell, matches, feathers, sage and sweetgrass. She set aside his water jug and glass and set out everything on his bedside table with castors. She'd completed a smudging ceremony for Sharon earlier and her new friend had appreciated it. Lydia intended to explain every aspect of the smudging as she carried it out.

"What a pretty feather!" Mrs. Chamberland exclaimed.

"Thank you. It's a tail feather from a red-tailed hawk. Many people use an eagle feather, but this is one of my favorites, a gift from my grandfather many years ago."

"And what is that?" Mr. Chamberland inquired, pointing.

"Sage. Along with tobacco, sweetgrass and cedar, they represent the first medicines of First Nations people."

"I've seen smudging ceremonies before," Warren piped up. "When I attended culinary school, one of the student chefs, Edwin, was a First Nations Cree from Saskatchewan. I'm still good friends with him."

Lydia continued, "Directing the smoke with this single feather will clean the aura in the room and around our bodies. The spirits of these sacred plants will cleanse and restore balance and centering. Through smudging we give thanks and show our gratitude, and pray for blessings for our life, for our family, and for our community."

Mr. and Mrs. Chamberland and Warren appeared extremely interested.

"This is a very spiritual process for my people with deep powerful meaning. It's difficult to explain." Lydia paused for a moment. "As a child, I was taught that we smudge our eyes that we may see good things in people, our hands that we may do good work, our minds that we may have good thoughts, and our hearts for our family and community. That explanation may help you to understand, too, but of course, its meaning goes much deeper."

"Dear, that does help." Mrs. Chamberland smiled at her, seating herself in the visitor's chair.

"My grandfather taught me how to perform the ceremony when I was barely a teenager." She paused in her preparations and met all three sets of eyes in turn. "I don't want to push my beliefs onto anyone. If you prefer, I could just—"

"Not at all. Please continue." Mr. Chamberland waved her on.

"I agree," Warren added, setting Lydia's purse aside and sitting on the edge of his father's bed.

Lydia continued, "I have a circle of braided sweetgrass at home, and I will bring it for your room next time."

"Thank you, Lydia," Mr. Chamberland replied.

"You're a very lovely young lady." Mrs. Chamberland's hands rested on her lap. "I can see why my son is so fond of you."

Lydia's eyes welled at their acceptance, encouraging her to honor her ancestors' traditions and beliefs. "As I mentioned, this is a very sacred ceremony for my people. I will begin with a prayer to the Creator."

*"O Great Spirit of our Ancestors, Creator of all things, hear my voice…"* Lydia spoke the prayer.

When she finished, she mixed pieces of sage and sweetgrass in the abalone shell presented to her by her mother and father on her thirteenth birthday. She struck a match and lit the mixture. A trail of smoke spiraled into the air as the spiritual mixture smouldered.

Lydia carried the shell around the room and directed the smoke to all four directions. Next she directed the smoke around Mr. Chamberland and encouraged him to use his hands to waft smoke over himself, cleaning his aura. She repeated the process with Mrs. Chamberland and then with Warren and finally herself. She immediately relaxed, feeling centered and at peace.

The pungent scent of sage and lingering sweet smell of sweet-grass hung in the air. She closed her eyes, the comforting scents familiar to her for as long as she could remember. As much a part of her upbringing as her education and family memories collected over her lifetime.

She opened her eyes and gazed at Mr. Chamberland who appeared more relaxed in his bed, body less rigid and eyes closed. He might not share her beliefs but he certainly appeared to have embraced the concept, emotionally at least. She knew without a doubt in her mind, in some way, the ceremonial benefits would aid in his healing and recovery.

She gathered up her smudging materials, and packed them away in a special pouch tucked into her purse. When she looked up, Mr. Chamberland had drifted off to sleep.

"That was wonderful. Thank you so much," Warren whispered, kissing her cheek.

"Now, we'll let Dave be, and I'm going to get a cup of coffee," Mrs. Chamberland whispered, and then walked Lydia and Warren to the elevator.

"How is Warren's brother doing?"

"Blaine contracted an infection after his two surgeries, but he is doing much better now. We're hopeful he'll be home soon." Mrs. Chamberland hugged Lydia and Warren again.

"I'm going to go visit Blaine for a while, Mom," Warren said, as the elevator door opened.

Lydia touched his arm. "Tell Blaine and Karen I said hello."

"I'll do that." Warren slipped his arm around her.

"Thank you again for coming." His mother stepped into the elevator and Warren and Lydia followed.

Lydia smiled. "You're very welcome. I was already here visiting the woman from the accident."

Mrs. Chamberland's eyes lit up. "Warren told me about that. I'm so proud of you."

Lydia's eyes filled, hearing the woman's praise. She'd only met her a couple of times, and for Warren's mother to say something so kind spoke volumes about her personality. "Thank you." She managed to get the words past the lump in her throat.

"You come and visit Dave and me again."

Lydia smiled. "I will. I hope the smudging helped."

"He's resting more peacefully than I've seen since he arrived here." She touched Lydia's arm. "I'm certain it helped. And thank you again."

Lydia nodded. "I need to get home to prepare for a very important date," she teased, winking at Warren.

The elevator door opened. "You both have a nice night," Mrs. Chamberland called as Lydia stepped out.

"I'll see you tonight. My truck is still at the dealership for repairs. You're picking me up outside the C-train station, right?" Warren added.

"You bet. Six o'clock. See you later." She playfully blew him a kiss as the elevator door closed.

FOUR O'CLOCK IN THE AFTERNOON, Lydia raced out of her bedroom to answer her mother's front door. Lydia had moved in for the summer months and she loved being out of the city for a while. As she entered the living room, her first cousin, Ernest, the Tsuut'ina police officer in the family, stepped inside. He was dressed in full uniform, looking serious and professional, his long jet-black hair neatly braided.

Had something happened?

"Has my lazy cousin been sleeping all day?" Ernest teased her, pointing to her silk bathrobe.

"No! And I am not lazy. I performed two smudging ceremonies in hospital today. Sharon and Warren's father." So much for worrying if this was an official visit.

"Good for you, cousin." Ernest smiled at her.

"I'm dressed like this because I had a shower. And I have a date tonight."

He nodded. "With the cooking guy."

"Warren is a professionally trained chef! Do not refer to him as 'the cooking guy'," Lydia blurted, despite knowing her cousin was again teasing her.

"If he cooks food for a living, he's a cooking guy." Her cousin headed into the kitchen and grabbed a cola out of the fridge.

Lydia trailed behind him. "Nobody is home but me. Why are you here?"

"Nice to see you, too. Hope everything has been okay with the family." He winked at her and tipped back the can, drinking deeply.

Lydia shook her head. Two years older, her cousin had been like this her entire life. They'd been close growing up, more like brother and sister. She knew he'd never change.

"We've been fine. Thank you for asking." Lydia turned on her heel. "If you'll excuse me, I need to do my hair."

"Guess you don't want this letter then."

Lydia froze in her tracks and turned back, meeting his eyes. What letter? Her mother had picked up their mail already today. There hadn't been any mention of a letter.

Ernest removed an envelope from his pocket and waved it at her.

"That's for me?"

He nodded. "Some police officer from the Calgary Police Service dropped it off. Said the person who wrote it was 'special circumstances' whatever that means. But the officer said he'd cleared it with his superior. He didn't know your address on the reserve, so requested we deliver it."

Lydia stood, stunned.

"So, I'm here delivering it." Ernest held out the envelope to her.

"Who is it from?"

He shook her head. "I don't know. Special circumstances. Read it."

Lydia retraced her steps and reached for the plain white envelope with her first name scrawled across the front in cursive handwriting. Who'd be writing her a letter? Sharon Robertson? Had something happened to the baby? No. The handwritten scrawl seemed likely written by a man.

"Open it. Can't be bad news or they would have insisted it be delivered immediately," Ernest reasoned, polishing off the cola.

"How long have you had it?"

"It was dropped off yesterday." Ernest shrugged. "I had the day off, so I'm here today."

Lydia hoped the contents weren't time sensitive, if the letter had lain unattended for a full twenty-four hours. She took a deep breath and ripped open the envelope, unfolding the two lined notebook pages inside.

"Anything important?"

"I don't know yet. How fast do you think I can read?" She met her cousin's eyes.

He shrugged.

Lydia smiled at him standing there, hands on hips. He appeared prepared to go arrest the writer if need be. He might tease her mercilessly, but he'd always had her back. She returned her attention to the letter and began to read…

Dear Lydia

My name is Steve Parker. You don't know me, but I need to write you this letter and I'm hoping you're gonna read it. I'm the guy who was driving the stolen Jeep.

I screwed up a lot since leaving my foster home. I started hanging out with other street kids, and we were doing okay for a while. Keeping to ourselves and avoiding the cops when we needed to steal food or something.

*Then I met a guy who promised me I'd make a lot of money. Kevin told me I'd be able to buy whatever I wanted. And I believed him. Yeah, I know. What an idiot, right?*

*He got me and a couple other kids into drugs, using and selling them, too. I never saw a penny for it. And he bought us booze. Big mistake. Especially the booze. My mom was an alcoholic and I think I'm the same as her.*

*Next thing I know, he had me stealing cars. Threatened to turn me into the cops if I didn't do what he wanted. He told me I was a nobody and no judge would believe any story I tried to tell. Seemed logical to me.*

*The guy beat me up a couple times when I refused to steal for him. It seemed safer, easier, to do what he wanted. And then the accident happened. Being arrested that night was probably the best thing that could have happened to me. That might sound crazy, but it's true. It might have saved my life.*

*After I was arrested, I gave the guy's name to the cops. Kevin was all we ever called him. I don't know if he's been arrested. I don't care. I never want to see him again.*

*I'm staying at a special house right now, and I have a public defender working on my court case. He hopes I won't go to jail, but I've never gotten a break in my life so I'm not holding my breath. At least I'm not constantly looking over my shoulder and wondering who might bash in my head or shoot me. I actually feel safe for the first time in months.*

*I wanted to thank you for saving that woman's life. I heard she was pregnant, so I guess you saved her kid, too. One of the cops told me she could have bled to death if not for you. I'm so glad you were there. I'm in a lot of trouble, but thanks to you I'm not facing a murder charge.*

*The cop told me you said you wanted me to get my act together. I wanted you to know that I'm trying. Yeah, that's all I wanted to tell you.*

*Steve*

Lydia's eyes welled with tears. What a nice gesture, writing her the letter. She didn't know the teen and she'd been furious with him at the time of the accident. But hearing his side of the story, she could understand how helpless he felt. Defeated, as if all of society was working against him.

"Cousin, do I need to go beat up somebody for you? Arrest somebody?"

"Ernest! I'm not ten and we're not on the school playground anymore." Lydia shook her head, knowing he was teasing. He would never risk the job he loved with such unprofessional, irresponsible behavior.

He laughed heartily. "So you're good here?"

"Yes," she replied, stuffing the letter into the envelope. "It's all good."

"I'm going back to work. Thanks for the cold drink." He strode across the floor and closed the door behind himself.

Lydia slumped onto the sofa. She still couldn't believe Steve's story. He didn't mention anything about a father. Perhaps he'd never known the man. At least, she'd had her father for the first sixteen years of her life. And two loving grandparents and extended family. She couldn't feel more fortunate for the life she'd been born into. And she understood her mother now, having talked with her about Stampede and honoring her heritage at Indian Village. Her mother only had Lydia's best interests at heart.

But this kid, Steve Parker. No wonder he'd ended up on Crowchild Trail that night.

Wrong place. Wrong time.

She didn't doubt for a minute he'd been forced to steal the Jeep that night, as he'd claimed. At least, Steve sounded sincerely remorseful for his actions. And he'd thanked her for saving Sharon's life.

In a way, Lydia had saved Steve's life also. Saved him from death on the streets, even if he did face a jail sentence. But she'd contributed to him receiving help for his issues with alcohol, and having been placed in what sounded like a half-way house. Giving him peace of mind in a safe environment for the first time in ages.

Maybe one day soon Steve would qualify for some kind of training, enabling him to land a decent job, completely turn his life around. Giving him a future as a contributing member of society. And all because she'd known what to do to save a complete stranger from bleeding to death.

Right place. Right time.

She smiled, once again completely convinced a career in nursing was her correct path in life. She couldn't wait for September, to begin her final year of training.

"Lydia, are you home?" Her mother called from the back entry.

"In the living room, Mom."

Her mother strode into the room. "I'm glad I caught you before you left. I have news for you."

Lydia settled on the sofa. "What news? Am I going to like this?"

"I'm taking my summer vacation the first three weeks in August."

"Okay…" Lydia waited for the punchline. Or a 'but'.

"And I want you to come with me."

Lydia's mouth dropped open. "What?"

"You told me you only have two more events booked to serve. I'd like you to resign and take the rest of the summer off before you return to school."

Lydia sighed. "Yes, I'm returning to school, but you have no idea how close I came to packing it in." She shared everything with her mother: the horrendous time she'd put in during her third year, including her crippling emotional trials, and her fears about not being good enough.

Her mother listened in silence.

Lydia grimaced. "Are you disappointed in me?"

"Not in the least!" Her mother settled beside her on the sofa. "When I was in training, our class had one student who was probably the worst nursing student ever. She failed several tests, she would forget to don gloves before procedures, and she'd constantly drop instruments."

Lydia shifted position, listening intently. This student sounded worse than her.

"But one semester, everything fell into place. Every one of her fellow students was shocked at the high marks she achieved, and her practical performance improved beyond comprehension. At training completion, she graduated with honors close to the top of her class."

"Wow! Maybe there is hope for me, too," Lydia whispered.

"I believe in you, my girl." Melanie winked at her daughter. "If I pulled off honors after the horrible times I had, anyone can."

Lydia gasped. "That was you?"

Melanie nodded. "And I've never looked back. If I'd quit after those dismal marks and dropping instruments, I wouldn't have enjoyed all these years working as a nurse. Imagine all the lives I've saved? All the babies I've helped bring into the world? None of that would have been possible had I quit."

"Remember the man in the restaurant? The guy who you saved by performing CPR until the ambulance arrived?"

"Heart attack." Her mother smiled. "I happened to be in the right place when it mattered. Just like the night you were driving down Crowchild Trail."

Lydia hugged her mom. "So, I'm resigning next time I work a catering shift. If we get time together, I'm not going to mind missing dance competitions. Tell me about this vacation you're planning for us."

"I'm renting a small motorhome we can handle easily. I've made reservations at a campground in B.C. for the first two weeks, and I've reserved a spot at a beautiful place at Banff for the last week. Just you and me. Hiking. Cooking outdoors. Campfires at night. Staring up at the stars and enjoying each other's company before you return to university in September."

"Can we go to Radium Hot Springs for a couple days?" Lydia playfully crossed her fingers.

Melanie laughed. "Absolutely!"

"Mom, you're the best. I can't wait."

"Won't you miss this boy you've been seeing? Warren?"

Lydia met her mother's eyes. "Yeah, I will. But you and I need this time together more. Warren and I can text."

"I agree. We'll have a wonderful time. Perhaps this will be the last time we can vacation together. Just the two of us." Her mom patted her leg.

Lydia glanced at the living room clock and leapt off the sofa. "I have a date with Warren tonight. I've got to hurry or I'll be late."

"Have fun," her mother called as Lydia dashed to her bedroom to finish getting ready.

## CHAPTER 22

Saturday evening after Stampede

*W*arren spotted Lydia's SUV parked outside the Stampede grounds where he'd finished a half shift and changed for dinner before heading to their agreed meeting place near the train platform. He hurried over so she wouldn't have to stop for long.

"Hi. Sorry, I'm a little late," he called through the open window before climbing into the passenger seat, clicking the seatbelt into place, and greeting her with a quick kiss.

"Hi. I just got here, not a minute ago." She pulled away from the curb. "Running a little late myself."

Warren settled in his seat, enjoying the breeze coming in through the window. Her vehicle was equipped with AC, but Lydia loved the fresh air.

"How was work?" She glanced over at him.

"Okay. I heard about the job." He paused for effect. "I got it."

"Warren! That's wonderful! It's not the Palliser, but next best to it." Lydia blinked rapidly.

"Don't you start crying. You're driving!" He warned her.

"I'm not crying." She rolled her eyes, playfully. "But I want to. I'm so happy for you."

"Emailed my resume four days ago, interviewed yesterday, and they called me an hour ago to say I'm hired." Warren couldn't wipe the smile from his face. "And I forgot to tell you at the hospital, that I got the stitches out on Wednesday." Warren stuck out his hand. "The doctor was shocked at how well it's healed. Still tender as heck but no infection. The doctor wasn't happy that I'd gone back to work so early, but probably because of it, I won't require any physio."

"More wonderful news!" Lydia exclaimed.

"Good as new before I know it. And I don't start the new job for two weeks, so it will have more time to heal." Warren rested his hand on her thigh. "I was so damn lucky. I won't be doing that again."

"Your career is too important to you."

"But not as important as you." Warren touched her arm. "How about you? Getting some sleep now that Stampede is over?"

"Sleep? People actually sleep?" she teased with mock surprise.

"Usually for seven or eight hours of completely non-productive time every night." He laughed. "But I hear you. Stampede is over for another year, but now with Dad and Blaine in the hospital, it's been crazy. The investigation is under way. Nothing definite yet as to what happened with the Cessna."

"Really?" Lydia glanced at him.

"Blaine was flying and he told me what happened. The plane stopped climbing and drifted left, clipping the left wing when it came down before landing on its nose. He's thankful the plane didn't burst into flames."

"Oh, my, I guess so!"

He nodded. "Blaine suspects something happened with the engine. Maybe not enough fuel reaching the engine or something. We're all going to wait for the investigator's report."

Lydia drove toward downtown in silence.

Warren still couldn't believe the generous gesture she'd done for his dad. His beautiful First Nations girlfriend never ceased to amaze him. He'd definitely lucked out the day he'd first spotted her during an event at the Lazy S. Of course, their collision had been a surprise, but maybe Fate worked at bringing people face to face in a shocking manner, especially when they were meant to be together, ensuring they got the message. Almost knocked on his butt, he'd gotten it all right. Good work, Fate!

"I saw Dad again after I talked to Blaine. Dad woke up a few minutes before I got there. He thinks you're cute and a keeper, by the way." Warren winked at her when her head whipped around and she met his eyes.

Lydia chuckled. "I must have made more of an impression than I thought. I'm happy he approved of the smudging."

"Mom and Dad are pretty open-minded when it comes to new stuff." Warren leaned back in his seat. "The scent of the sweetgrass still lingered in the air when I was there the second time. Pretty relaxing actually. There's something to the 'getting rid of the negative energy' you told them about."

Lydia smiled. "I appreciate their open-mindedness."

"How is Sharon? Mom mentioned you'd seen her."

"Counting the days until her baby arrives. According to her husband, she doesn't do sitting around all that well." Lydia laughed. "Mike bought her two dozen magazines to keep her occupied, and I brought her three romance novels. Hopefully, the nurses are able to keep her in bed!"

Warren laughed. "Bring her a book with those number puzzles in it. Those would keep me busy for weeks. I have a heck of a time figuring them out."

"Sudoku? I love those! Good idea. I'll bring Sharon some." Lydia stopped at a red light and met his eyes. "You won't believe what happened today."

While wending her way through early Saturday evening traffic, she told him about the letter she'd received from Steve Parker.

"Wow. Sounds like he actually regrets everything he's done. Maybe there's hope for the guy after all."

Lydia smiled at him. "I agree. I hope someone gives him a break."

"And being bullied by that Kevin character. I hope the police figure out who he is and make him pay for every rotten thing he's done to Steve and kids like him."

"Wouldn't that be nice? Getting the guy behind bars and off the streets so he can't take advantage of any more down-on-their-luck street kids." Lydia smiled.

"Maybe sic your cousin on him. He sounds like he'd be more than pleased to arrest the guy. Remind me to behave myself when I'm on Tsuut'ina land." Warren grinned. "I'd hate being arrested."

"The Tsuut'ina Police Service is an excellent police force. A female member won the 2017 Officer of the Year award from the First Nations Chiefs of Police Association for her work."

"I'm impressed."

"Neither of us has anything to worry about. Law-abiding citizens that we are," Lydia declared. "Remember when you told me to saddle a dream and ride it to success?"

Warren nodded.

"I hope Steve does the same. But enough about him." Lydia smiled. "We're going to the Calgary Tower. I've never been there, unless with my parents as a child. If so, I don't remember."

Warren laughed. "I haven't been there in years. But I made a reservation, and we're going so I can spend some of my casino winnings, spoiling you with a wonderful, extravagant dinner."

"You don't think that going there for dinner is too touristy?"

"Absolutely not!" Warren reached over and gave her hand a quick squeeze. "Lots of Calgarians go to the Sky 360 Restaurant. My parents often take out-of-town friends there. It's a great idea."

Lydia sighed. "Okay. Your dad did mention that the food was excellent."

"Dad's right. I want to read their menu and sample some of the dishes."

Lydia chuckled. "Check out the culinary competition?"

"Exactly. We have a dinner reservation. We'll order a drink and gaze out over the city and consider our future. We'll discuss anything you want to about *us*."

"Okay." She stopped at another red light.

Warren leaned over and kissed her. *Us.* He liked the sound of that. He couldn't believe she'd forgiven him, after how badly he'd hurt her. But he wanted a future with her more than anything. The light changed and she accelerated away. She was an excellent driver.

Warren glanced out the car's side window. "You drive downtown? It can get pretty crazy."

"Emily visited the tower recently and she mentioned her date parked in the Palliser parkade. Apparently, it's handy."

"Nick?" Warren ventured.

"Yep. They're getting pretty cozy. Might be serious." Lydia reached the parkade a few minutes later.

Warren pointed out a vacant spot. After acquiring a ticket for the parked vehicle, they headed into the tower lobby.

"I've only got a couple more events in July and then I'm resigning from Stampede Catering for the remainder of the summer."

"Dancing competitions?" he ventured.

Lydia shook her head. "Mom's taking her vacation time and she's renting a small motorhome. I'm so excited. We're going camping together, just the two of us, for three weeks before I return to school."

"Three weeks! That's great." Warren frowned. "For you! I'm going to miss talking to you and seeing you every week."

Lydia thought for a moment. "We can text and Facetime on our phones. We'll be in B.C. for two weeks and a week in Banff."

"I wish I could take a week off and join you, but when I start the new job, that's out of the question."

"I guess it wouldn't hurt to ask."

"No, I've landed this dream job, I'm not about to start slacking already." Warren shook his head. "We've got years to be together."

Lydia hugged his arm. "I like the sound of that."

# CHAPTER 23

*L*ydia and Warren arrived at the entrance to the tower. Lydia stepped inside when he held the door for her. Always the gentleman.

"We have a reservation under Warren Chamberland," he said.

The woman behind the desk checked and verified the name. "Yes, here you are. Enjoy your evening. As well as dinner, access to the observation deck is included for free." She smiled and directed them toward the elevators.

They stood arms linked in the enclosed elevator as they ascended. Lydia stared at the video images of the 360-degree view surrounding the tower, digitally displayed on the walls. Warren wrapped her in a tight embrace and nuzzled her neck. His beard tickled her skin. She smiled and her arms circled his neck. "I hope I'm dressed okay," she whispered.

"You look amazing in this dress." Warren played with the ruffle on the collar of her pink floral sundress. He buried his hands in her hair, leaned closer and inhaled deeply. "Man, I love that citrus scent in your hair, when it teases my nose." He met her eyes. "Restaurant management might frown on my dark jeans and plaid shirt. Haven't gotten completely out of Stampede mode yet."

"Well, this is Calgary." Lydia smiled.

The elevator halted when they reached the top floor observation deck.

"I would love to kiss you right now, but those doors are going to open right away."

Lydia stood on tiptoes, pecked his lips. "Take a risk once in a while, Chamberland," she whispered seconds before the door opened.

Warren laughed. "You never cease to surprise me."

"Keeps guys on their toes." She exited the elevator.

He followed. "Guys?"

"Cousins. Grandfather. Guys." Lydia strode across the carpet and stepped onto the area of glass floor along a portion of the edge. She peeked over the side through the window.

Warren followed but stopped a step or two short of the glass floor.

Lydia looked over her shoulder. "Chicken?" she whispered loud enough for him to hear.

"Hey." Warren took a tentative step forward. "Just needed a moment."

"Praying before facing certain death?" she teased.

He grabbed her around the middle, tickling her ribs. She squirmed out of his hold.

"Actually, you shocked me by stepping right onto that floor. I figured I'd spend twenty minutes convincing you it was perfectly safe."

Lydia peeked around him. "One, two, three, four, five…"

"What are you doing?" Warren looked behind him.

"Counting how many people are *already* standing on the glass floor." Lydia grinned. "I figured it was safe enough."

"Logical." Warren looked down over the busy street below. "This is some view."

"The people look so small! The cars resemble toys little boys play with."

"There goes the C-train." Warren settled his arm on her shoulder. "I think that curved building in front of us is called Bow Tower."

"It's beautiful," Lydia gushed. "Such a unique design."

Warren and Lydia moved along to the right.

"Isn't that multi-level building City Hall?"

"Yep." Warren guided her alongside him. "Look. There's the Saddledome and Stampede grounds!"

"I see the oval track that the chuckwagons race on," Lydia added. Her phone pinged a notification while she was taking a picture. She read the text. *In labor. Baby eager to make an appearance. Husband is nervous wreck.*

"Oh, my goodness. It's from Sharon. She's in labor!"

"Already?"

"She's only a couple weeks early. And who knows, maybe her dates are off a bit. There shouldn't be any problems if the baby is born now," she speculated. "Gosh, this is exciting."

Lydia replied. *Good luck. Tell him everything will be fine. Will visit you guys tomorrow.* She received a happy face emoji in return.

After a few minutes, they moved farther along the curved observation deck.

"Look at the mountains! And the sun shining off them. Isn't that a gorgeous sight?"

Warren slipped his arms around her. "As stunning as you," he whispered, nuzzling her neck.

"Sweet talker." She giggled. "Look at all these buildings. Office towers. Apartment complexes. They're so much taller than the tower."

"I know. Maybe there's an unofficial competition to build the tallest building." Warren laughed.

Lydia considered the possibility he was speaking a truth. Soon after looking west and spotting the Olympic Park and the ski hill in the distance, she led him back to the starting place across from the elevators.

"I'm starving." Warren squeezed her hand. "But first I've been dying to do this."

Lydia gasped when he pulled her into a tight embrace. And then she smiled, realizing his intent. Her eyes closed when his warm lips found hers. His facial hair tickled again, but she didn't mind. Whatever aftershave brand he wore, the crisp spicy aroma sent her pheromones into overdrive.

A minute later, Lydia broke the kiss, fearing they would be putting on an X-rated show if this kept up. And several children were wandering the observation deck with their parents.

"We need to eat. Now," she whispered.

"Spoil sport."

"Preferable to being arrested for an indecent PDA," she countered, laughing at his frown. "Public display of affection."

Warren nodded. "Ah. Wise decision. Let's go eat."

Warren pulled open the door near the elevator, allowing Lydia to enter first. They climbed the steps leading to the restaurant. Warren spoke with the woman at the check-in desk outside the restaurant and another woman directed them to their table.

Lydia peeked out through the window at the city spread before her, setting her purse on the window ledge. "I wonder how long it takes for the restaurant to revolve all the way around?"

"About an hour." Their server stood, smiling. "And I wouldn't set my purse there, unless you don't plan on seeing it again for another sixty minutes."

Lydia grabbed her handbag and set it on her lap. "Oh my goodness! Thank you for warning me." She smiled at the woman dressed in black with an apron wrapped around her middle.

Warren exchanged pleasantries with the woman who then inquired, "What can I get you folks to drink?"

"A glass of white wine for me, please," Lydia piped up.

Warren caressed her hand. "I'll have a Caesar, please, the spicier the better."

The server set a menu in front of each of them and recited the evening's specials. "I'll be right back with your drinks." She headed off to another table.

"Thank you for bringing me here," Lydia said, electrical charges racing up her arm with each caress.

Warren winked at her. "This place is great. And perfect for a date."

The server arrived with their drinks and they gave her their order. "I'll be right back. Your appetizers shouldn't take too long."

Warren raised his glass to Lydia. "A toast."

Lydia reached for her wine goblet. "What are we toasting to?"

"You choose."

Lydia smiled. "To us."

"Simple and perfect." Warren chuckled and clinked glasses with her. He gazed into her beautiful eyes while they sipped their drinks. "Now, what will we talk about?"

Lydia shook her head. "Nothing. Anything. Tonight, I don't have a care in the world. I want to enjoy the view and the company."

Shortly after the waiter cleared their entrée dishes, Lydia's phone pinged again. She read the text. *Baby here. Sharon and son doing fine.*

She squealed. "Sharon's husband texted me. She had the baby!"

Warren set his glass down. "Wow! What has it been? A couple hours? That was fast."

"Yeah, especially for a first baby, but it happens. Thank goodness she was already in the hospital. And her husband says both of them are fine."

"That's great news."

Lydia glanced at her phone and burst into tears.

Warren straightened in his seat. "Oh, no. What happened?"

Sharon shook her head and handed him her cell, tears streaming down her face. The text read *We're naming him Lynden to honor the woman who saved his life.*

Warren smiled at her from across the table. "That's fitting. You did save both of them."

Lydia dug a tissue out of her purse and dabbed her eyes, smiling. She couldn't be more shocked or more honored. "I know, but I didn't expect that. We'd joked that she would have to wait until she had a daughter to name her Lydia. Tomorrow, I'm going shopping and I'm buying Lynden the biggest teddy bear I can find."

Warren laughed. "I need to meet Sharon and warn her that you'll have her son spoiled rotten before he leaves the hospital."

She laughed. "You're probably right."

Warren raised his glass. "A toast. To Lynden."

Lydia clinked glasses with Warren, her eyes dry again. "To sweet little Lynden."

They took a sip, smiling across the table at each other.

"Now, where were we?" Warren set his glass down. "Right, earlier you suggested we enjoy each other's company tonight. I couldn't agree more. I want to learn more about you. Tell me your deepest darkest secrets."

Lydia laughed. "I wouldn't know where to begin."

"I doubt that. You're too fun-loving and genuine. I doubt you have one." Warren winked at her. "Now, on the other hand, I could go on for hours."

"You're much too focused on your goals to have time to get into trouble." Lydia tilted her head. "Unless there was a misspent youth I'm not aware of."

Warren shook his head. "Nope. Too busy on the ranch for mischief-making. Except for that one incident involving my brother, a case of beer and the riding mower."

Lydia leaned forward in her chair, smiling. "Do tell."

Warren grinned at her. "Maybe I'll tell you some time. Or ask Mom about the year the perennial beds took a beating."

When he grinned at her like that, her heart melted. She never wanted to lose him or his quirky sense of humor. Or his warm personality. She'd found the man for her. She took his hand in hers.

"Promise me, when we're old and gray and reliving our youth, we'll still enjoy exchanging stories of all the silly things we did when we were young."

"We'll be facing the future together, forever and ever," Warren speculated.

"You can bet your favorite frying pan we will," Lydia said, kissing him.

Warren chuckled. "Works for me, beautiful."

Love the novel you just read?
Your opinion matters.
Review this book on your favorite book site, review site, blog, or your own social media properties, and share your opinion with other readers.
Thank you.

# NOTE TO READERS

Lydia Simpson-Crowchild, Melanie Simpson-Crowchild, Bernard Crowchild and Ernest Crowchild are fictional characters, completely born of the author's imagination.

However, David Crowchild (1899-1982) served as chief for the Tsuut'ina Nation from 1946 to 1953. Formerly part of the Morley Trail, Crowchild Trail was named in his honor in 1971 by the city of Calgary. For over thirty years, the Chief David Crowchild Memorial Award has honored an individual or group's contributions to cross-cultural experiences and understanding.

In one scene in this book, there is a smudging ceremony performed in a patient's room in the Foothills Hospital. While Alberta Health Services makes every possible effort to accommodate First Nations patients, ceremonies would not be performed in the patient's room. Many hospitals set aside a special 'culture room' for sacred First Nations ceremonies, including smudging. Thus, I have taken artistic license in writing the scene.

*Brenda*

Canadian readers…
To assist STARS Air Ambulance in flying
accident victims to hospital, please use the link below
to make a donation to this life-saving foundation.
Thank you so much for your help!
https://foundation.stars.ca/AB-donatenow

# BANNOCK RECIPE

Ingredients:
    4 cups all-purpose flour (or whole wheat flour or combination)
    4 tablespoons baking powder
    1 teaspoon salt
    1/2 cup of shortening
    2 cups warm water or milk
    1 cup berries (optional)
Directions:
Mix together flour, baking powder and salt in a large bowl.
Cut in the shortening until it makes a nice crumble.
Gradually add water or milk to make a soft dough.
Add berries if you choose.
Knead on the counter for 3  5 minutes, then shape into a ball.
Place ball on a greased baking sheet and flatten with your hands into a circle or rectangle about 1 inch thick. Prick with a fork.
Bake 400 deg. F. for approximately 30 to 35 minutes or until lightly browned.
Slice into squares. To serve: cut a square in half and spread with butter. For a treat also spread with jam.

WOMEN OF STAMPEDE SERIES

Saddle up for the ride! The Women of Stampede will lasso your hearts! If you love romance novels with a western flair, look no further than the Women of Stampede Series. Authors from Calgary, Red Deer, Edmonton and other parts of the province have teamed up to create seven contemporary romance novels loosely themed around The Greatest Outdoor Show on Earth... the Calgary Stampede. Among our heroes and heroines, you'll fall in love with innkeepers, country singers, rodeo stars, barrel racers, chuckwagon drivers, trick riders, Russian Cossack riders, western-wear designers and bareback riders. And we can't forget our oil executives, corporate planners, mechanics, nursing students and executive chefs. We have broken hearts, broken bodies, and broken spirits to mend, along with downed fences and shattered relationships. Big city lights. Small town nights. And a fabulous blend of city dwellers and country folk for your reading pleasure. Best of all, hearts are swelling with love, looking for Mr. or Miss Right and a happily ever after ending. Seven fabulous books from seven fabulous authors featuring a loosely connected theme—The Calgary Stampede.

WOMEN OF STAMPEDE BOOKS

Hearts in the Spotlight, Katie O'Connor
The Half Mile of Baby Blue, Shelley Kassian
Saddle a Dream, Brenda Sinclair
Eden's Charm, C.G. Furst
Unbridled Steele, Nicole Roy
Betting on Second Chances, Alyssa Linn Palmer
Trick of the Heart, Maeve Buchanan

# ABOUT BRENDA SINCLAIR

Brenda Sinclair is the author of over twenty historical western romance and contemporary romance novels. After a career in the accounting field, she traded in numbers for words to become a full-time novelist. She is a contributing member of her local romance association where she supports and mentors other writers, believing in paying it forward by helping others.

Brenda has been married to her husband for over forty-five years. During this time, they have raised two sons and welcomed three wonderful grandchildren.

When Brenda isn't writing, she's walking her little dog Kelly, checking out what Jack Abbott is up to on The Young and The Restless, or reading a great book!

Brenda believes life is good, and for days that life isn't so good, just get over it. There's always tomorrow.

Contact Brenda Sinclair
Website: http://www.brendasinclairauthor.com
Email: mailto:brendasinclairauthor@gmail.com

facebook.com/brendasinclairauthor

twitter.com/bsinclairauthor

Made in the USA
Columbia, SC
23 June 2018